# FIGHT TO THE DEATH

Clint drew swiftly and fired at Lanigan. The bullet shattered Lanigan's right collarbone, numbing his arm so that the gun dropped from it.

Myles had his gun out, but Goodnight was firing, and although his shots were going wild, they were enough to attract Myles's attention. Clint took advantage of the situation and fired at the man. His bullet struck Myles square in the chest, punching right through his breastbone and driving all of his breath out of him . . .

# DON'T MISS THESE
## ALL-ACTION WESTERN SERIES
# FROM THE BERKLEY PUBLISHING GROUP

***THE GUNSMITH by J. R. Roberts***
> Clint Adams was a legend among lawmen, outlaws, and ladies. They called him . . . the Gunsmith.

***LONGARM by Tabor Evans***
> The popular long-running series about U.S. Deputy Marshal Long—his life, his loves, his fight for justice.

***LONE STAR by Wesley Ellis***
> The blazing adventures of Jessica Starbuck and the martial arts master, Ki. Over eight million copies in print.

***SLOCUM by Jake Logan***
> Today's longest-running action Western. John Slocum rides a deadly trail of hot blood and cold steel.

# THE GUNSMITH

## 144

### WEST TEXAS SHOWDOWN

## J. R. ROBERTS

JOVE BOOKS, NEW YORK

WEST TEXAS SHOWDOWN

A Jove Book / published by arrangement with
the author

PRINTING HISTORY
Jove edition / December 1993

All rights reserved.
Copyright © 1993 by Robert J. Randisi.
This book may not be reproduced in whole
or in part, by mimeograph or any other means,
without permission. For information address:
The Berkley Publishing Group,
200 Madison Avenue,
New York, New York 10016.

ISBN: 0-515-11257-7

A JOVE BOOK®
Jove Books are published by The Berkley Publishing Group,
200 Madison Avenue, New York, New York 10016.
JOVE and the "J" design are trademarks belonging to Jove Publications, Inc.

PRINTED IN THE UNITED STATES OF AMERICA

10  9  8  7  6  5  4  3  2  1

# THE GUNSMITH

### 144

## WEST TEXAS SHOWDOWN

# ONE

When Clint Adams rode into Lubbock, Texas, he was tired. He had ridden his big, black gelding, Duke, hard through much of New Mexico over the past few weeks, and all he wanted from Lubbock was a rest stop before he continued on to Labyrinth, Texas.

He put Duke up at the livery, with instructions to the liveryman for special care.

"Don't worry, mister," the man said, "an animal like this *deserves* special care."

Duke was getting on in years, but he was an impressive beast, nevertheless.

Clint only wished he could say the same thing for himself.

"You can't be serious about this, Charles," Fred Canby said.

"I'm very serious, Fred," Charles Goodnight said.

The two old friends were sitting at a table in

the Americana Saloon, enjoying a glass of whiskey and a cigar each.

"But bringing in more wire . . ." Canby said, shaking his head.

"The wire is necessary, Fred," the cattleman insisted.

"Maybe a *fence* is necessary, Charles," Canby said, "but *barbed* wire—"

"You've been reading too many horror stories, Fred," Goodnight said. "Barbed wire is not the scourge of the West, as the Eastern newspapers have been making it sound."

"Perhaps not," Canby said, "but there are enough of your neighbors who think it is. Hell, you've already had encounters with Sessions and Taylor," Canby said, naming two of Goodnight's closest and biggest neighbors.

"Frank Sessions is a fool," Goodnight said. "He thought he could abuse my hospitality, and he tried it once too often."

"You and Frank used to be friends, Charles," Canby pointed out. "Since the wire—"

"It's *not* since the wire," Goodnight said, jabbing at the air with his lit cigar. Goodnight was a big, barrel-chested man with dark hair going gray in streaks. At the moment he was wearing a three-piece gray suit, but he was more at home in his trail clothes.

"My dispute with Sessions started when he got greedy," Goodnight explained. "He started to abuse the use of my land, and the water that I was allowing him to use. It's because of that abuse that he and I are at odds, *not* because of the wire."

"If you took down the wire," Canby said, "rather than putting up more—"

"Forget it, Fred," Goodnight said. "My wire is up to stay, and I've brought more in. It'll be going up as soon as I get it back to Palo Duro Canyon."

Goodnight's ranch sprawled throughout the Palo Duro Canyon, between Lubbock and Amarillo. He had neighbors, but none of them had as much land as he had. For years he had allowed his neighbors to graze on his land, until men like Frank Sessions began to abuse the privilege.

"You're asking for more trouble, Charles," Fred Canby said, shaking his head. "More trouble than you need, believe me. . . ."

Goodnight pinned his longtime friend with a hard stare and asked, "Is that a threat, Fred?"

"Oh, not from me, Charles," Canby said. "It's not a threat, it's . . . a warning . . . or a prediction, if you prefer. I only wish you'd listen to reason—"

"Fred," Goodnight said, leaning forward in his chair, "I know you don't like the barbed wire. In fact, I recognize that you are an ardent detractor of it, but don't let that put us on opposite sides."

"Believe me, Charles," Canby said, "the last thing I want to do is end up on the, uh, opposite side of the fence from you."

"Good," Goodnight said. He stood up and looked down at his friend. "I have to get going. I've got miles of wire to string."

Canby watched sadly as his friend left the saloon.

• • •

As Clint walked past the general store, he saw a buckboard out front. It appeared to be loaded with rolls of barbed wire. Clint had not been following the controversy over the wire, but he was well aware of its existence. Curiosity caused him to cross the street to get a better look at it.

Standing by the buckboard, he touched the hard, sharp ends of the short wire points. He could see where the points could tear up a cow—or a man. He could also see, however, where the wire would act as a deterrent.

"Can I help you?" someone asked from behind him.

He turned and saw a man standing there, staring at him, possibly as curious about him as he was about the wire. The man was in his late thirties, wearing worn trail clothes. He wore a gun, but Clint had the feeling he was much more at home with a lariat.

"No," Clint said, "sorry, I didn't mean to—I was just curious, that's all. I really haven't seen the wire up close before now."

"You a cattleman?" the man asked.

"No, no," Clint said, "I just got into town and was on my way to the saloon. I saw the wire and I'm afraid my curiosity got the better of me."

"This here is Mr. Goodnight's wire," the man said. "He don't want nobody messin' with it."

"Fair enough," Clint said, putting his hands up. "I was just looking. I'll be on my way."

"That's a good idea, mister," the man said.

Clint waved and walked away from the buckboard. The last thing he needed was to get into some sort of confrontation just moments after arriving in town.

That was when he heard the first shot.

# TWO

Clint turned and saw two men. One was the man he had just spoken to. He was no longer standing, but lying on the ground.

The other man was wearing a suit with a vest. He was crouched behind the buckboard with a gun in his hand. It only took Clint a moment to realize that no one had shot at him, but at the man he'd been talking to. As two more shots rang out, he saw that the man in the suit was now the target.

Clint drew his gun and tried to locate the source of the shots. When two more shots were fired, he saw where they were coming from. Somebody was on the roof of a nearby building, using a rifle to fire down at the man by the buckboard.

The man in the suit fired back, but his aim was off. He struck the front of the building, but that was all. Clint decided to lend a hand because he hated bushwhackers.

He ran to the side of the man in the suit and said, "I'll cover you. Get your man to safety!"

The man looked at him for a moment, as if trying to decide what his stake was in the matter.

"Pull him to safety!" Clint shouted, and then fired up at the man on the roof. His shot came considerably closer than that of the man in the suit, and the bushwhacker ducked down for cover.

"Now!"

The other man moved quickly, grabbing the fallen man beneath the arms and pulling him to safety behind the buckboard.

The man with the rifle stood to fire again, but Clint dissuaded him with another shot. He thought he heard someone cry out, and then the man disappeared from view.

"How is he?" Clint asked.

"He doesn't look too bad," the other man said, "but he needs a doctor."

"Then get him to one," Clint said. "I'll check the roof."

"All right."

Clint left the cover of the buckboard, but the rifleman on the roof did not reappear.

Clint quickly located the building the man had been firing from and ran inside. He found himself in a woman's clothing store. The clerk, an attractive young woman with black hair, looked at him, startled. The customer she was waiting on actually cried out and put her hand to her mouth. She was considerably older than the clerk.

"I'm sorry," he said, "but someone is firing shots from your roof. How do I get up there?"

The clerk reacted immediately, shrugging off her surprise in a way he admired.

"Through here," she said, indicating a curtained doorway behind her, "and up the stairs."

"Thanks."

He hurried behind her counter, brushing against her as he passed. He went through the curtained doorway and found the stairs.

He was fairly certain he had hit the bush-whacker on the roof, but since he didn't know whether the man was wounded or dead, he ascended the stairs carefully. When he reached the second floor, he looked for a hatch in the ceiling and found it easily because it was open. There was a chair just beneath it, which made it obvious how the man had gotten up there. The question now was—was he still there?

He stood on the chair and had to holster his gun in order to reach up and pull himself up. He knew he was putting himself in a vulnerable position, and took a moment to wonder why before hauling himself up and through the open hatch.

When he was through, he rolled on the rooftop, clawing for his gun at the same time. He came to a stop with the gun held out ahead of him and quickly scanned the roof.

He was alone.

The shooter was gone.

He took a moment to examine the roof and

found some bloodstains by the front, where the man must have stood while firing. Satisfied that he *had* wounded the man, but apparently not badly enough to keep him from getting away, Clint started back to the street.

# THREE

Clint was coming out from the curtained doorway when a man with a gun entered the store. In a split second he saw the man's badge and managed to put his hands in the air, holding his gun in his right.

"Take it easy!" he called out.

He didn't want to get shot by a nervous or overzealous lawman.

"Just keep your hands up!" the lawman shouted.

"They're up."

The female clerk was standing off to one side, watching the two of them with wide eyes. She did not, however, look frightened.

"Sheriff," she said finally, "I think you're making a mistake."

"We'll see about that, Miss Garfield," the man with the badge said. "Drop that gun," he told Clint.

"I'm going to lay it down," Clint said. "Dropping it could do some damage to it or cause it to go off."

"Just set it down real easy," the man with the badge said.

At that moment, as Clint was setting his gun down, the man dressed in the suit came in.

"No, no, Sheriff," he said testily, "not *that* man. He's the one who helped me."

The sheriff looked confused.

"I . . . didn't know . . ."

"I tried to tell you," Miss Garfield said.

"Sheriff, you'd better go out and try to find that shooter," the other man said.

"You might try around back," Clint said. "He might have dropped down from the roof. I wounded him, so you might also look for some blood."

"Well, Sheriff?" the man said.

"I'm goin'," the sheriff said.

The lawman went out the door, and the man in the suit looked at Clint.

"He's useless," he said. "Pick up your gun, mister. I'm beholden to you."

Clint picked up his gun and said, "I just have a habit of poking my nose where it doesn't belong."

"Lucky for me," the man said. "My name is Goodnight, Charles Goodnight."

Clint frowned.

"The Goodnight who blazed the Goodnight-Loving Trail?" he asked.

Goodnight looked embarrassed and said, "My partner and I did that, yes."

"Well, it's a pleasure to meet you," Clint said, shaking the man's hand.

"Would you let me buy you a drink?" Goodnight asked.

"I don't see why not," Clint said. "Just let me talk to the young lady a moment."

"I'll wait outside," Goodnight said.

When Goodnight was gone, Clint turned to the woman and took a good look at her. She was extremely pretty, wearing a white lace blouse with a high collar and a long black skirt.

"Ma'am, I'd like to apologize if I frightened you," he said.

"That's all right," she said. "I gather from what I heard that you saved Mr. Goodnight's life."

"That's possible," he said. "There's no telling what would have happened if I had minded my own business."

"I don't think you'll convince Mr. Goodnight of that," she said.

"May I ask your name?" Clint said.

"Alicia Garfield."

"I'm Clint Adams, Miss Garfield," he said. "I'd like to do something to make up for the intrusion."

She looked surprised and said, "Sir, are you . . . asking me to . . . to . . ."

"Go to dinner with me, yes," Clint said. "It will be my way of apologizing."

"As I said before," she said, "there is no need."

"But you do eat dinner, don't you?"

"Well . . . yes," she said, looking amused.

"Then perhaps we could eat it together?" he said, pressing the issue.

Looking even more amused, she said, "I . . . hardly know you."

"Then we'll have a long dinner," he said, "and

by its end we'll know each other a lot better. What do you say?"

"Well . . ."

"Good," he said, "I'll call for you here. What time do you close?"

"At seven."

"Then I'll be here," he said, and left before she could protest.

Outside he found Charles Goodnight waiting for him.

"Might I ask your name, sir?" Goodnight said.

"Clint Adams, Mr. Goodnight."

Goodnight stared at him and said, "You mean . . . the Gunsmith?"

"I've been called that, yes," Clint said.

"Well, sir," Goodnight said, "this is a pleasure. Come, I'll take you to the finest saloon in town for the libation of your choice."

He'd hardly been in town half an hour and already he'd been involved in a shooting, made the acquaintance of a rather famous man, *and* a lovely young lady.

Lubbock was turning out to be much more than he'd bargained for.

# FOUR

Goodnight took Clint to the saloon he had just left Fred Canby at, the Americana. It was more than a saloon, really. It was a full-fledged gambling hall, with enough gaming tables to entertain the whole town—or so it seemed to Clint. The ceilings were high, and the bar was polished mahogany. Once upon a time you only saw establishments like this in San Francisco or New Orleans. Now they were spreading all over the West, to Lubbock, El Paso, Dodge City, Tombstone, and Virginia City.

As they entered, Clint thought Goodnight was looking around for someone, but he didn't comment.

In truth, Goodnight was checking to see if Fred Canby was still there, and was satisfied to see that the man wasn't.

"Let's get a table," Goodnight said. "One of the girls will bring us a drink. What'll you have?"

"Just a beer," Clint said. "As a matter of fact, I

14

just rode in under an hour ago, still haven't had anything to cut the trail dust."

"The beer's cold here," Goodnight assured him. "You'll enjoy it."

They sat at a back table, and as Goodnight had predicted, a saloon girl came over and asked what they would like. Clint had the feeling he would not have gotten such service had he not been in the company of Charles Goodnight.

"Two beers, Brenda, please," Goodnight said.

"Yes, sir," she said, and for a moment Clint thought she might execute a slight curtsy.

"You, uh, don't own this place, do you?" Clint asked Goodnight.

"Oh, no—you mean the service?"

"And the respect."

"Well, I'm in here quite a bit when I'm in town," the man said. "They know me here."

Clint didn't know if he meant at the saloon, or in the town, but then decided that both probably applied.

"You don't live in town, then?"

"Oh, no," Goodnight said, shaking his head. "I have a spread in the Palo Duro Canyon, north of here. It's between here and Amarillo. I have some property in New Mexico and Colorado, as well, but my primary concern these days is the Palo Duro spread."

"I noticed the wire—" Clint said, and then stopped when Brenda returned with the drinks.

"Will there be anything else, Mr. Goodnight?" she asked suggestively. "For you *or* your friend?"

"Not right now, Brenda," Goodnight said. "We'll

let you know if there is, though."

As Brenda walked away, Goodnight watched her and then said to Clint, "Not what you'd call pretty, but fetching as all hell, wouldn't you say?"

"I would," Clint said. He had noticed that the blond Brenda, though not particularly pretty as Goodnight had pointed out, did indeed have a "fetching" quality to her. Clint was a firm believer that women did not have to be beautiful to be attractive or sexy. Brenda seemed a perfect example of the type.

However, the woman in the store, Alicia Garfield, was another matter entirely. . . .

"Drink up, Mr. Adams," Goodnight said, lifting up his mug. "I'd like to drink to the health of the man who saved my bacon."

Clint raised the mug in return and then took a healthy drink.

"I was saying I noticed the wire," Clint went on. "Talked to your man, in fact, just moments before the shooting. How is he, by the way?"

"I'll check on him when we're through here," Goodnight said. "I think he'll make it, although he won't be doing any work for me for a while."

"Was the shooting related to the wire, do you think?" Clint asked.

Goodnight put his mug down and eyed Clint with interest.

"Why do you ask that?"

Clint shrugged.

"It was a bushwhacking," Clint said, "pure and simple. That means someone with a grudge. I understand that this barbed wire has been known to bring the worst out in some people."

"That it has," Goodnight said. "Some of my neighbors have exhibited some bad feelings about my using the wire myself."

"You think this was one of your neighbors' doing?" Clint asked.

"I didn't see the man who was doing the shooting," Goodnight said, "not that it would have mattered if I had. He was probably just a hired gun."

"Probably."

"You hit him, you say?"

"I did," Clint said. "There's some blood up there on the roof."

"Well, maybe you slowed him down enough for that good-for-nothing sheriff to catch up to him," Goodnight said sourly.

He was playing with his beer more than he was drinking, turning the mug around in circles over and over again. Some of the beer had sloshed over onto the table and his hand, but he didn't seem to notice.

"Don't think much of the local law, I gather?" Clint asked, taking another long sip from his beer after the remark.

"Humph," Goodnight said, snorting in disgust, "there's an election coming up soon, and I'll be backing a man against him."

Clint didn't say anything. It seemed to him that with a man like Goodnight behind him any man would be able to get into office rather easily. He'd been to many towns where the sheriff was in some rich rancher's pocket. He wondered if Goodnight was the kind of man who wanted *that* kind of a sheriff.

"Say," Goodnight said, leaning forward, looking at Clint with keen interest now, "you wouldn't be interested in a job, would you, Clint? It's all right if I call you Clint, isn't it?"

Clint frowned across the table at the man, considered both questions, and wondered which of them he should answer first.

# FIVE

"I'm not really looking for a job, Mr. Goodnight," Clint said, "and of course you can call me Clint."

"And you have to call me Charles," Goodnight said. "Don't misunderstand me, please. I was not offering you the *sheriff's* job. What I was referring to was you coming to work for me, on my ranch."

"I'm not much of a ranch hand."

"No, no," Goodnight said, "I'm still not making myself clear."

"Charles," Clint said, very slowly, "I don't hire out my gun."

Goodnight studied Clint for a few moments, and then sat back. He took his hand away from the beer mug he'd been playing with.

"Let me change directions here, Clint," he said finally. "I'm certainly not trying to offend you in any way. If I have, I'm sorry."

"It's all right."

"Do you mind if I ask what you're doing here in Lubbock?"

"Passing through," Clint said. "I just stopped here so my horse and I could get some rest."

"Excellent!" Goodnight said, obviously pleased.

"I'm sorry?"

"My ranch is a perfect place for you to rest," Goodnight said. "I'd like to invite you to come out . . . as my guest, naturally."

"Well," Clint said, "that's very generous, Mist— I mean, Charles, but—"

"May I point something out here?"

"Please do."

"The chances of you getting any rest here in Lubbock are very slim."

"Why is that, Charles?"

"Well, as you said, you were hardly here an hour and already you've managed to take sides."

"I didn't take any sides."

"I'm sorry, but you did. When you stood beside me out there, you took sides."

"That's absurd."

"I agree," Goodnight said, "but how do you think the rest of the town will look at it? First you help me, and then we come to the saloon together— not that I planned this, Clint!" the man hurriedly added. "I'm simply pointing out how it must look."

Clint saw that the man was right.

"Keep going."

"Whoever sent that gunman after me is also going to think that you've sided with me," Goodnight said. "They might be after you next, wanting to get you out of the way before they come after me again."

Another point well-taken, Clint thought.

"Well then . . ." Clint said, "I could just leave town."

"Exactly what I'm proposing," Goodnight said.

"I mean leave and head south."

"To where?"

Clint hesitated a moment, then said, "To wherever I was headed."

"All right," Goodnight said, "never mind where you're headed. That's none of my business. Finish your beer. Would you like another?"

"No," Clint said. "I think I'd like to check into the hotel and get some rest."

"Of course, you're right," Goodnight said. "Look, when I leave here I'm going to check on my man and then head back to the ranch."

"Alone?"

"I have other men here in town."

"I see. . . ."

"I'll leave you directions to my ranch," Goodnight said. "If you change your mind, you can ride out and you'll be welcome. How's that?"

"That's fine," Clint said.

"Good."

They left the saloon together and stopped on the boardwalk outside.

"I want to thank you again, Clint," Goodnight said. "You did me a service today I will not soon forget."

"I was glad to help."

"I won't shake your hand," Goodnight said. "Not out here, anyway, with people watching—"

"Don't be an ass," Clint said and put out his hand.

Goodnight beamed, accepted the hand, and pumped it vigorously.

"I hope to see you soon," Goodnight said. "If not, then sometime in the future. You'll always be welcome."

"I appreciate it, Charles."

They parted company there, Goodnight walking back toward his wagon and Clint headed for the hotel.

Clint knew Goodnight was right. Anyone who had witnessed his assistance of the man would take that as a sign of a side taken. Their public handshake just now would also foster that impression. There was nothing he could do about that, though. He decided not to worry about it, that there was no reason for him to put himself on guard.

He spent his life that way, anyway.

# SIX

Fred Canby regarded the wounded man with an annoyed expression on his face. They were in Canby's office, on the second floor of the brick City Hall building. The man had entered through the rear door, so that no one would see him. Even though he'd done that, Canby was incensed that he had come to the building. More than that, though, Canby was angry that the man had failed to do what he was being paid to do—kill Charles Goodnight.

"You're an idiot!" he snapped. "I should have known better than to hire you."

"Mr. Canby," the man began, holding his wounded arm. Blood seeped through his fingers, but Canby ignored that totally. "The other man—" he tried to continue, but Canby cut him off.

"I don't want excuses," Canby said. "You were hired to do a job and you didn't do it."

"I got the other man—"

"A ranch hand," Canby said, "and you didn't

23

even kill *him*. He's recovering. In other words, Murphy, you're a total failure."

Murphy frowned, more at Canby's words than at the pain in his arm.

"Does that mean I ain't gettin' paid?"

"Oh, you're getting paid, all right," Canby said bitterly. "You're getting paid to get the hell out of town—and out of Texas! Don't ever come back, either."

"What about my arm?" the man said. "I need a doctor to look at—"

"You'll live until you get out of Texas. Find a doctor in Oklahoma, or New Mexico."

Canby took an envelope out of his desk drawer and handed it to Murphy. It was the money he was supposed to have been paid to kill Charles Goodnight.

"I don't care which direction you ride in, just get the hell out of town and out of Texas. Do you understand?"

"Sure, Mr. Canby," Murphy said, taking the envelope in his good hand. It immediately soaked up the blood from his wound. "I understand."

"In case you don't," Canby said, "let me make it clearer. If you come back to Texas, I'll have *you* killed."

"S-sure, Mr. Canby," the man stammered, "I under—"

"Get out!" Canby said. He turned his back on the man to stare out his window at the main street below.

He heard the door open and close and the echo of the man's footsteps as he walked away. Moments later he heard the door open and close again, but he had heard no approaching footsteps. That always amazed him about Hank Lanigan.

He turned and saw Lanigan standing in front of his desk, looking as taciturn and impassive as ever. He employed Lanigan because the man never let emotion get in the way of his job. In fact, Canby had never seen Lanigan exhibit emotion of any kind.

"Follow him," Canby said. "When he's far enough out of town, kill him and get my money back."

"Right."

Lanigan turned and started for the door. He stopped with his hand on the knob.

"What is it?" Canby asked.

"What about Goodnight?"

"Don't worry," Canby said. He turned to look out the window again. "I have other plans for Charles Goodnight."

Clint walked to the hotel, entered, and checked in. He was on the steps to the second floor when it hit him.

If Charles Goodnight had more men in town, where were they while the shooting was going on?

"Damn it!" he said.

To the surprise of the desk clerk, Clint ran back down the stairs, out the front door, and headed for the livery stable.

# SEVEN

When the buckboard carrying the barbed wire stopped, Goodnight frowned. He had been riding behind it while one of his men drove the wagon and the other two flanked it. Now that they all had stopped he rode on ahead.

"What's wrong?" he asked. "Why have you stopped?"

"Sorry, Mr. Goodnight," one of the mounted men said. Goodnight was shocked to see that the man was pointing a gun at him.

"What's going on?"

"Just sit your horse easy, Mr. Goodnight," the other man said.

Goodnight turned and saw that the second man was pointing a gun at him as well.

"Traitors!" he said, understanding what was happening. "How much were you paid?"

"A lot of money," said the man on the buckboard. His name was Ayres. On Goodnight's right was Fenner, and on his left, Holcomb.

"I'll double it," Goodnight said.

"No you wouldn't," Ayres said. "You'd never forget this, and you'd hold it against us."

To Goodnight's way of thinking, none of these men had worked for him for very long.

"Well, at least you've worked for me long enough to know that," Goodnight said. "So, which one of you will it be?"

"Which one of us will . . . what be?" Ayres asked.

"Which of you will pull the trigger and kill me?" Goodnight said.

Ayres looked puzzled. He had yet to produce his own gun.

"We're not gonna kill you, Mr. Goodnight," he said. "We're only supposed to take you someplace—you and the wire."

"And I'll be killed there."

Ayres didn't say anything.

"Or are you naive enough to think that I wasn't going to be killed at all?" he asked the three men. "Come on now. You men must know that you are to be, at the very least, a *party* to murder. Accomplices!"

The three men exchanged uncertain glances.

"Well, I won't wait for that," Goodnight said, "so you had better be ready to use your guns now."

"Mr. Goodnight," Ayres said, "don't do anything foolish. Take out your gun and drop it on the ground."

"I'll do no such thing," Goodnight said. "In a moment I'm going to draw my gun and shoot the lot of you—that is, unless you shoot me first."

"Don't force us—" Ayres said.

"Take him!" Holcomb shouted.

Goodnight heard shots even as he went for his gun, even as he knew he'd be too late, but he was damned if he'd go meekly to his death without taking *somebody* with him.

Odd, though, that he hadn't been shot yet. . . .

Clint rode hard until he saw the wagon and the men around it. Two of them were pointing guns at Goodnight, and if he read the man right he wasn't about to go anywhere willingly.

He heard one of the men shout and, cursing, he drew his gun and started firing.

To Goodnight's surprise, Holcomb, the man who had shouted, fell from his saddle. Goodnight had his gun out by then, and as he turned to look at Fenner, the man went flying from his horse as if he'd been yanked off from behind.

Goodnight looked at Ayres, who was going for his gun.

"Don't, son."

Ayres ignored him. He grabbed for his gun, and Goodnight fired. His bullet took Ayres in the face and knocked him from the buckboard.

Goodnight turned as he heard a horse behind him and was surprised to see Clint Adams approaching him, gun in hand. It was only then that he realized what had happened to Holcomb and Fenner.

"Saved my bacon again, huh?" Goodnight asked.

"We'd better check them," Clint said, dismount
ing.

He went to each man and examined them, sat-
isfying himself that they were dead.

"They all work for you?" he asked Goodnight.

"They did."

"For how long?"

"Not very long."

"They say who hired them?"

"No," Goodnight said, "only that they were paid
a lot of money."

"To kill you?" Clint asked.

"They said no," Goodnight replied. "They said
they were supposed to take me someplace—me
and the wire."

"The wire," Clint said, nodding.

"What brings you out here to save my life again?"
Goodnight asked.

"I got to thinking," Clint said. "I remembered
you said you had other men in town, and I was
wondering where they were when the shooting
was going on."

"So you assumed they had been paid off?"

"It seemed a safe bet," Clint said.

"And you figured I'd never get to my ranch
alive," Goodnight said.

"That also seemed a safe bet."

"Well," Goodnight said, "as it turned out, *they*
didn't make it. I'll have to go it alone from here."

"No," Clint said, "I'll ride along with you."

"You'll work for me?"

"No," Clint said, "I'll *ride along with you*, and
maybe take you up on your offer to rest at your

place for a while—but that's all."

"That's enough," Goodnight said. "Let's get started."

"No," Clint said again. "Tomorrow."

"Tomorrow?" Goodnight repeated. "Why tomorrow?"

"Because you may not have much respect for the lawman in Lubbock," Clint said, "but we still have to have some respect for the law. We'll have to take these men back to town and explain what happened to the sheriff. After that, we can head for your ranch."

"Very well," Goodnight said reluctantly. "I suppose you're right."

"I know I am," Clint said. "Now, you want to step down and help me collect these bodies?"

# EIGHT

Clint drove the wagon back into Lubbock, with Goodnight riding alongside. Trailing behind were Duke and the horses belonging to the dead men. There was one dead man slung over one horse and two on the other.

They went directly to the sheriff's office and found the man behind his desk.

"Did you find that son of a bitch who shot at me?" Goodnight demanded as they entered.

The sheriff leapt to his feet, almost knocking his chair over.

"I found some blood behind the building, like this fella said," the lawman said, "but I wasn't able to find anybody."

"Well, we've got three somebodies outside for you," Goodnight said.

"What?"

"Outside," Goodnight said, staring at the man.

Goodnight and Clint went outside with the sheriff trailing behind curiously.

"What the hell—" the man said when he saw the bodies on the horses. "Who were they?"

"My men," Goodnight said. "Some son of a bitch paid them off."

"Who?"

Goodnight gave the man a disgusted look.

"If I knew that, I would have told you," he said impatiently.

"Unfortunately," Clint said to the sheriff, "we weren't able to keep one of them alive so he could tell us."

The sheriff looked at Clint and said, "Say, just who are you?"

"His name's Clint Adams, that's who he is," Goodnight said. "He's going to be my guest for a few days."

"Adams?" the sheriff said.

"Are you still checked in at the hotel?" Goodnight asked Clint.

"I am."

"Well, I guess I better take a room."

"You're stayin' in town tonight?" the sheriff asked Goodnight. The man looked surprised.

"We'll be getting an early start in the morning, Sheriff," Goodnight said. He turned to Clint and asked, "Will you take the wagon to the livery?"

"Sure," Clint said, reasoning that he had to take Duke back over there anyway.

"I'll see you at the Americana later," Goodnight said, "after I check in."

"Charles," Clint said, "don't you think you should keep a low profile for a while? I mean, there have been *two* attempts on your life in the past couple of hours."

"I know that," Goodnight said, "but I'll be damned if I'm going to hide my head."

"I'm not saying you have to hide," Clint said, "just don't go walking around by yourself."

"What do you suggest?"

"Check in at the hotel and wait for me there," Clint said. "We'll go to dinner."

Goodnight thought a moment, then nodded and said, "All right."

"And you're buying," Clint added.

Goodnight laughed, slapped Clint on the back, and said, "I *insist* on buying!"

Goodnight went off, still laughing, leaving Clint with the sheriff.

"Who killed these men?" the lawman asked.

"I killed two, and Goodnight killed one," Clint said. "They didn't leave us any choice."

The sheriff looked at Clint curiously.

"How long have you worked for Mr. Goodnight, Adams?" he asked.

"I don't work for him," Clint said. "If you heard him, he said I was his guest."

"How long have you known him?"

"A couple of hours."

"You make friends fast, don't you?"

Clint smiled at the man and said, "I'm just a friendly guy, Sheriff."

He untied the two horses bearing dead men from the back of the wagon.

"That ain't the reputation I know," the sheriff said.

Clint handed the reins to the man and said, "Then don't believe everything you hear, Sheriff."

Fred Canby spent many of his days staring out his window. In his youth he had spent most of his days in the saddle but, unlike Goodnight, he had moved onto other business endeavors. Some days, however, when he was just looking out the window, he wished he was back in the saddle once again.

Canby was looking out the window when Clint Adams and Charles Goodnight rode back into town, bringing with them three dead men. He stared at them, shaking his head.

It looked as if he was going to have to take more drastic measures to achieve his goals.

First, though, he was going to have to find out who the hell that other man was.

# NINE

Clint found Charles Goodnight waiting impatiently for him in the hotel lobby.

"Did you get a room?" Clint asked.

"I did," Goodnight said. "Are you ready to eat?"

"As soon as I put my saddlebags and rifle in my room," Clint said.

"Well, get to it, then," Goodnight said. "I'm famished."

"It'll just take me a minute," Clint said.

"Go, go, go," Goodnight said impatiently.

When Lanigan returned to Fred Canby's office, his face was as impassive as ever. Canby knew that Lanigan could have returned from killing a family of five and he would *still* look that way.

"Is it done?"

As his answer Lanigan produced the envelope of money Canby had given Murphy. It was smeared with blood. He dropped it on the man's desk, where Canby allowed it to stay.

"All right," Canby said. "Goodnight is back in town."

"How?"

"He brought three dead men in with him, that's how," Canby said.

"Goodnight killed all three men himself?" Lanigan asked.

"No," Canby said, "he had help."

"Who helped him?"

"That's what I want you to find out," Canby said. "Tonight."

"All right."

"Don't *do* anything, Lanigan," Canby said. "Just find out who the man with Goodnight is, and let me know. After that, I'll tell you what to do. Understood?"

"Understood."

"All right, then," Canby said, "go."

Lanigan was the perfect employee, Canby thought. The man was like a gun. You pointed him and he went off when you pulled the trigger—and he *never* asked questions.

# TEN

Goodnight took Clint to a small restaurant he would never have found on his own. The man was greeted the same way he seemed to be everywhere in town, as if he owned the place.

"Respect," Goodnight said, but Clint had to wonder if it really was respect, or fear.

They were shown to a table by a waiter who asked Goodnight if he wanted beer.

"Yes," Goodnight said, "we both do . . . and the beef stew."

"Yes, sir."

As the man walked away, Goodnight said, "They don't serve beer here."

"So how are we going to get it?" Clint asked.

"They'll send someone to the saloon for it," Goodnight said.

"Because they respect you so much."

"Right."

Clint nodded to himself.

"I hope you don't mind that I ordered for both of us," Goodnight said, "but the beef stew is exceptionally good here."

"That's fine."

"Besides," Goodnight added, "I want you to have the best. You saved my life not once, but twice today. Would you consider accepting some sort of reward?"

"No."

"Money, or—"

"No, nothing."

"I was going to say, perhaps a horse? I have some fine stock—"

"I have a horse."

"Yes," Goodnight said, "I couldn't help but notice. It's a magnificent beast. Too bad it's a gelding. Was it difficult to handle? Is that why you gelded it?"

"He was already gelded when I got him," Clint said. "I don't know why."

"Probably difficult to handle," Goodnight said. "It's the most common reason."

"Tell me about the barbed wire," Clint said suddenly.

Goodnight looked surprised.

"What about it?"

"I don't know," Clint said. "Its history, the different types."

Goodnight spoke briefly about the beginning of the wire, then went off on a long discussion of the different types. Clint heard names like Ellwood Ribbon, the Winner, Corsicana Clip, Split Diamond, Knickerbocker, Burnell's Four

Pointer, Necktie, Tack-Underwood, Brotherton
Barb, Brink Flat, and Buckhorn.

Basically, there seemed to be two types, two-
point and four-point.

"I prefer a four-point wire myself," Goodnight
said. "It's the most effective, and it's difficult to
unwind. My preference is the Brotherton Barb.
That's the one in my wagon now."

"You seem to have made quite a study of the
wire," Clint said.

"I think it's an important invention," Goodnight
said, "and when I decided to use it, I wanted to
make sure I got the best."

By now they had their beer and their dinner
and were almost done with both. Goodnight called
the waiter over and asked for two more beers.

"He doesn't have to do that," Clint objected. "We
can go to the saloon after this and have one."

"All right," Goodnight told the man, "forget it.
Just clear away the dishes."

"Yes, sir. Coffee?"

Goodnight looked at Clint, who nodded.

"Yes," Goodnight said, "for both of us."

The waiter brought a fresh pot and two cups
and poured for both of them.

"Tell me something about yourself," Goodnight
prompted.

"There's not much to tell."

"What about your reputation?"

"What about it?"

"Is it warranted?"

Clint hesitated. He didn't like talking about
himself, but he was to be a guest in Goodnight's

house, and the man seemed interested.

He talked briefly about his earlier days, when he first discovered how good he was with guns—not only shooting them, but taking them apart, putting them back together, fixing them, modifying them.

"Wait a minute," Goodnight said at one point, holding up his hand. "You're telling me that you came up with the double-action weapon before Colt did?"

"I suppose."

"My God! You could have been rich if you'd patented it!"

"I suppose," Clint said again.

"Aren't you—doesn't that bother you?"

"No," Clint said.

"Are you telling me that you don't want to be rich?" Goodnight asked.

Clint thought a moment, then said, "I suppose I wouldn't turn down the opportunity if it was offered to me, but I don't have any regrets."

Goodnight shook his head, but simply said, "Go on."

Clint talked about being a lawman for a while, and then of becoming annoyed at the way townspeople looked at their local lawmen. Finally, he told Goodnight about outfitting his own gunsmithing wagon and riding around the country for the past several years.

"So, you actually work as a real gunsmith?" Goodnight asked.

"Sometimes."

"Where's this wagon now?"

"It's in Labyrinth, Texas," Clint said. "I didn't need it this trip."

Goodnight nodded, digesting the information as he poured them each another cup of coffee.

"So . . . what about all the stories?"

"What stories?"

"About the men you've killed."

Clint hesitated, and then said, "I've killed men when it was necessary. I suspect the same is true of you."

"Yes, but I don't have a reputation for that."

"You do have a reputation though, right?"

"Yes."

"Is it totally deserved?"

Goodnight studied Clint for a few moments, then said, "Hmm, I see what you mean."

# ELEVEN

Lanigan entered the sheriff's office without announcing himself with a knock. The sheriff looked up from his desk and stared at him. He knew Lanigan was a hard case who sometimes worked for Fred Canby, who was a big man in town. The lawman wasn't necessarily afraid of Lanigan, but he *was* afraid of Canby—and so, by extension, he was *leery* of Lanigan.

"Lanigan," he said, nodding.

At first Lanigan had intended to go to the hotel to find out who the man with Goodnight was, but since the man and Goodnight had returned to town with dead bodies, that meant they had talked to the sheriff. This seemed a more direct course of action.

"Sheriff," Lanigan said, "I notice Goodnight came back into town toting some bodies."

"That's right."

"Had some help killin' 'em, did he?"

"He did."

"I was wonderin'," Lanigan said, "who that help came from. You know, who that other fella was?"

The sheriff hesitated a moment, then said, "Who was wonderin', Lanigan, you or Mr. Canby?"

Lanigan shrugged.

"What's the difference, Sheriff?" he said. "I'm doin' the askin' now."

They matched stares, and the sheriff was the first to avert his eyes, damning himself for doing so.

"His name's Adams," the man said finally, "Clint Adams."

"Clint Adams," Lanigan repeated. "You mean, the Gunsmith?"

"That's right, Lanigan," the sheriff said, looking back at the man now to see his reaction, "I mean the Gunsmith himself."

If the sheriff was expecting Lanigan to appear frightened by the news, he was disappointed. The only look that came over Lanigan's face was one of interest.

"Well," Lanigan said finally, "what do you know about that?"

"You find that interestin'?"

"Sheriff," Lanigan said, moving toward the door, "I find that *very* interestin'."

"You think Mr. Canby will find it—" the sheriff started, but before he could finish his question, Lanigan was out the door and gone.

# TWELVE

After they finished their coffee, Clint and Goodnight went once again to the Americana Saloon. It was crowded now, in full swing, but Goodnight still managed to find an empty table in the back. Brenda, the saloon girl from earlier, was at their side as soon as they sat.

"What'll it be, gents?" she asked.

"Beer," Goodnight said. She looked at Clint, and he nodded.

"Comin' up."

As she walked away—watched closely by Clint, Goodnight, and every other man close enough to watch—Goodnight said to Clint, "She likes you."

"That's nice to know."

"She's available, you know," Goodnight said. "All the girls here are."

"That's okay," Clint said. "I don't like paying for a woman."

Goodnight chuckled and sat back in his chair.

"Don't have to, eh?" he said. "You do all right for yourself?"

"I don't get lonely much," Clint admitted.

"Me," Goodnight said, "I've got a wife waiting for me at home. I get lonely when I'm away from her."

"That's nice," Clint said.

"Ever thought about getting married?" Goodnight asked. The question surprised Clint, caught him off guard.

"Once."

"What happened?"

"She got killed."

"Oh," Goodnight said, "I'm sorry."

"It was a long time ago."

"Still," Goodnight said, "it's a bad memory."

"That it is," Clint said.

Brenda returned with the two beers, set them on the table, then looked at Clint and gave him her best and brightest smile.

"Anything else?"

"Not right now," Clint said.

"You'll let me know if there is?"

"First thing," Clint promised.

She put her hand on his shoulder for just a fleeting moment, said, "Good," and walked away.

"Woman like that," Goodnight said, "she knows when she's being watched."

Clint nodded.

"Yep," Goodnight said, lifting his beer, "she likes you."

• • •

They talked about a lot of things that night. Some more about barbed wire, some about politics, gambling, women, the "old" days.

After several hours—and more than several beers—Goodnight sat back in his chair and said, "Well, time for this fella to turn in. I'd like to get an early start in the morning. That all right with you?"

"I have no objection," Clint said. "Let me walk you back."

"Oh, no," Goodnight said, waving him away. "That's nonsense. I don't need my hand held."

"There were two attempts on your life today, Charles," Clint said.

"Which you don't have to remind me of," Goodnight said, "but with two failed attempts, what are the odds there will be a third one tonight? I think it's more likely they'll lay low for a while before they try again."

"Well," Clint admitted, finding logic in what Goodnight was saying, "you have a point there."

"Good," Goodnight said, "then I'll see you at first light, in the lobby."

"Right."

Goodnight stood up and said, "You can keep drinking all you want. It will go on my tab."

"Thanks," Clint said, "but I'll probably finish the one I have and turn in myself."

"Suit yourself," Goodnight said. "I'll see you in the morning."

Clint watched Goodnight wend his way through the crowd until he went out the door. He picked up his beer to finish it when someone sat down across from him.

It was the saloon girl, Brenda.

"Well," she said, eyeing him boldly across the table, "I thought he'd never leave."

# THIRTEEN

On the way to his hotel Brenda made it quite clear to Clint that she expected no money from him.

"If you offer me some," she said, holding onto his arm, "I'll get very insulted. I'm not doing this for money."

"Why are you doing it?" Clint asked.

"Isn't that obvious?" she asked. "I like you. Isn't that a good enough reason?"

He smiled and said, "It always has been for me."

She entered his room ahead of him and then turned and came into his arms even before he could close the door. They groped at each other's clothes, removing them frantically, and then fell onto the bed in a tight embrace, arms around each other, bodies pressed together, kissing passionately. She moaned as his hands moved down her back to cup the smooth flesh of her buttocks.

Her hands roamed all over him knowingly,

touching him lightly beneath his testicles, cupping him firmly, and then stroking him until he was incredibly hard. That done, she slithered down between his legs and began to work on him with her talented mouth. He rolled onto his back to make it easier for her, and she crouched there between his legs, sucking him and stroking him at the same time. When she sensed that he was near exploding, she stopped, straddled him, and took him inside of her. She rode him that way while he reached up to touch her breasts and her nipples, and before long she moaned out loud, a moan that escalated into a near scream as he exploded inside of her. . . .

Later, as she was lying on her left side, he pressed himself against her, sliding one hand around to touch her belly and her breasts. His penis, hardening, lengthening, fit very nicely into the cleft of her buttocks. When he reached down between her legs to touch her, she quickly became wet. His fingers manipulated her expertly until her eyes were shut tightly and she was groaning, her body growing taut.

She reached behind her then, found his penis, spread her legs, and guided him into her from behind. She lifted her right leg high, draping it over his hip, and he moved inside of her that way, slowly at first, and then faster, his hand still stroking her in the front. The dual stimulation soon drove her over the edge, and he followed closely. . . .

•   •   •

Later, they talked while lying side by side. . . .

"Are you friends with Mr. Goodnight?" she asked.

"I wouldn't say that."

"Working for him?"

"No."

"Then . . . what?"

"I just happened to be in the right place at the right time, Brenda . . . twice," he explained.

"Will you be staying in town?"

"Tomorrow I'll be going back to Goodnight's place with him."

"To work for him?"

"No," he said. "Just to see that he gets there safely, and to stay as a guest for a few days."

"And then?"

"And then," he said, sliding a hand over her flat belly, "I may be back through this way."

"May be?" she asked, as his finger slid into her and made her wet.

"Yes," he said, "maybe."

As his fingers moved over her, she arched her back and said, "Oh God . . . I guess maybe will have to be good enough . . . for now!"

# FOURTEEN

The next morning Fred Canby awoke in his large house at the southern end of town. He had this house, and he had a ranch on the outskirts of town. The ranch was not nearly the size of Charles Goodnight's, but Canby knew that it could be if he wanted it to be. He had other interests, though, aside from ranching, which was what separated him from Goodnight. It was what made him the better man.

At the ranch he also had a wife, a woman he had grown increasingly more tired of over the past few years. For that reason he spent most of his time in town, at this house, with a variety of young women warming his bed for money. Oh, he had no illusions about that. He was in his fifties, he was not an attractive man, and there was no way any of these women would be in his bed were he not Fred Canby, with the power and money that he had.

The girl in bed with him this morning was all

of twenty-five. Lying on her back with the sheet gathered around her waist, she seemed to be all pear-shaped breasts and tousled black hair. Luckily, with this one he had been able to perform, and perform quite well, even if he did say so himself. Of course, having her on her hands and knees, with her impressive butt hiked up in the air, pleading with him to "give it to her" had helped a lot.

At his age he often needed extra added incentive.

Clint awoke first, with Brenda lying on his left arm. He flexed the fingers of that hand experimentally and knew that he still had some time before it began to grow numb. At that point he'd have to try to slide it out from beneath her without waking her. For now, he was content to lie there with her head on his arm and the length of her body pressed against his. He put his other hand behind his own head and stared at the ceiling.

He was having second thoughts, not only about riding out to his ranch with Goodnight, but about then remaining as a guest. Granted, he was somewhat curious about what the ranch would look like, but he'd gotten himself into all kinds of trouble in the past trying to satisfy his curiosity.

Still, what else did he have to do? If he didn't go with Goodnight, he would simply ride back to Labyrinth, Texas, and wait for another good reason to leave there. Most likely, he'd end up bored and start back out on the trail *looking* for reasons.

And he'd gotten himself into all kinds of trouble in the past in the name of *not* being bored, hadn't he?

It all boiled down to keeping his word to Goodnight, and at least seeing that the man—and his wire—got safely to his ranch.

Canby slid from the bed without waking the woman. He pulled on a dressing gown and went downstairs. He could smell the coffee in the kitchen, and he knew that the cook would be working on his breakfast now. Canby was confident that he had the best cook in Texas working for him, even if it was a man.

He entered the kitchen and saw Miraflores standing at the stove.

Raphael Miraflores was forty-six years old and had worked for Canby for many years. How many, each man had forgotten. As far as Fred Canby was concerned, Miraflores was the only person in the world he could trust, besides himself.

"Good morning, Raphael," Canby said as he entered the kitchen.

"Good morning, sir," Miraflores said. He spoke English with only the faintest hint of a Spanish accent. Miraflores was from Spain, and not from Mexico, so when he spoke Spanish it was true Castilian Spanish.

"What's for breakfast?" Canby asked.

"Flapjacks, sir," Miraflores said, "made with honey, and bacon."

"Very good."

Miraflores turned to face his employer. He was a

slight man with slicked down black hair parted
in the center and a very carefully tended mus-
tache—so carefully tended that it was hardly
noticeable.

"Will the lady be staying for breakfast, sir?"
Miraflores asked.

"I doubt it, Raphael," Canby said. "I doubt it."

Miraflores poured a cup of coffee and handed it
to Canby.

"Thank you, Raphael," Canby said. "I'll go
upstairs and wake the young lady and send her
on her way."

"By the time you return," Miraflores said,
"breakfast should be ready."

"Good," Canby said, "very good."

Clint stepped out of his room, closing the door
gently behind him. He'd inform the desk clerk
that Brenda was asleep inside and was not to be
disturbed. He'd pay an extra day for the room so
she could sleep.

As he started down the hall, the door to
Goodnight's room opened and a woman stepped
out. She had red hair, still disheveled, and
the front of her dress was not quite closed.
Clint was able to see the cleavage between
her creamy breasts. She noticed him, giggled
behind her hand, and hurried down the hall to
the stairs.

Clint stopped at Charles Goodnight's room,
put his ear to the door, and listened. He
heard movement inside, probably the man getting dressed.

So much for being a married man and lonely for his wife.

Canby sat at the kitchen table and ate his breakfast. He knew that Goodnight and his new crony, Clint Adams, would be leaving early for Goodnight's ranch in the Palo Duro Canyon. He did not have to be in his office, looking out the window, to know that. Very soon now they'd leave their hotel and be on their way. If Lanigan had done his job right, someone would be trailing them, keeping an eye on them for him until he decided what to do.

He had no problem with allowing the wire to reach the ranch, but he was not about to let Charles Goodnight string it. No sir, before that happened he'd come up with a plan and put it into effect successfully—Gunsmith or no Gunsmith.

Clint waited down in the lobby for Goodnight, who appeared in ten minutes. He was impeccably dressed, with every hair in place.

"Good morning," he said.

"Morning," Clint said. "Sleep well?"

"Very well," Goodnight said, "which is a surprise, since I hate being away from home."

"And your wife?"

"Especially my wife," Goodnight said. "A wonderful woman."

"I'm sure," Clint said.

He decided not to tell Goodnight that he had seen the woman leaving his room.

"Are we ready to get under way?" Goodnight asked.

"As soon as we get to the livery, get the team hitched up, and my horse saddled," Clint said.

"Well, then," Goodnight said, "let's get to it. I'm anxious to get back home."

# FIFTEEN

The ride to Goodnight's ranch was a one-day trip on horseback. With the wagonload of wire, it was a two-day trip, at best.

The first day passed uneventfully, which was a welcome change from the day before.

"We'll camp over the next rise," Goodnight said as early evening approached. "There's a water hole there. We can water the horses, fill our canteens, and wash up."

Since Goodnight had made the trip many times before, Clint did not question the man's choice of campsites.

They topped the rise, and Clint saw the water hole. There were indications around it of old camp fires.

Goodnight was driving the wagon, with Clint riding alongside on Duke. They went down to the water's edge and stopped. Goodnight applied the brake and dropped down to the ground.

Clint dismounted and said, "I'll scout up some firewood."

"I'll get the coffee out," Goodnight said. "Since we're only to camp one night, I'm afraid all I brought to eat is beef jerky, but there's plenty of coffee."

"Sounds good enough," Clint said.

"Besides," Goodnight said, "there'll be a fine meal for us when we get to the ranch. Count on that."

"I'll get the wood," Clint said, "and then tend to the horses."

"I'll unhitch the team in the meantime," Goodnight said. "Have to do my part, right?"

Clint had the feeling that Goodnight didn't often do much around a campsite except give orders. Of course, he could have been wrong. The man couldn't have built up the ranches that he had without doing some hard work. Maybe he was just far removed from those times.

Clint decided to give him the benefit of the doubt.

"We've got company," Clint said when they were seated around the fire, each with a cup of coffee in one hand and a piece of jerky in the other.

The horses had been taken care of, with special attention given to Duke. Once he had been sure that the black gelding was well taken care of, he had gone to join Goodnight at the fire.

"What do you mean?"

"Someone's been following us all day," Clint said.

"How do you know?"

"Well," Clint said, "first I could feel it, and then I spotted him."

"When?"

"About midday."

"And what's he doing?"

"Just following us."

"Alone?"

"Yes."

"What do you think he wants?"

"Well, since he's alone," Clint said, "I don't think he's going to come after us. I mean, if he was intending to kill us, he's had a clear shot many times."

"So if he's not out to kill us, then what?" Goodnight asked.

Clint shrugged.

"I suppose he's just keeping an eye on us," Clint said.

"For who?"

"That's a good question," Clint said. "One that maybe you can answer."

"I have a lot of enemies, Clint," Goodnight said. "I've made many over the years."

"What about now?"

"Now?" Goodnight asked. "You mean, right now?"

"I mean the wire," Clint said. "Who doesn't want the wire to go up?"

"Most of the people around here don't," Goodnight said, "but I think that's because they can't afford to put it up themselves."

"Why are you putting it up, Charles?"

"Because," Goodnight said, "it's an idea whose time has come. The open range is a thing of the past, Clint. These days you have to take land and make it yours, and the way to do that is to keep others off of it."

"And so, the wire."

"Yes," Goodnight said, "the wire."

They finished their meager meal and put on a fresh pot of coffee.

"So what do we do?" Goodnight asked. "About the man on our trail, I mean."

"Nothing, for now," Clint said. "He knows where we're going. That's no secret, so there's no harm in letting him follow."

"We could grab him and find out who he works for," Goodnight said.

"If we tried that now, he'd see us coming," Clint said. "We'd never reach him."

"You're good with a gun, right?" Goodnight said. "Couldn't you just . . . pick him off from here?"

Clint gave Goodnight a stern look.

"Never mind," Goodnight said, "forget I said it. We'll just let him follow us. What harm can he do if he's just doing that?"

"Right," Clint said. "Sooner or later we'll find out who he works for—that is, if you can't figure it out yourself before then."

"We?"

"What?"

"You said sooner or later *we'll* find out who he works for."

"Oh," Clint said. "Well, that's just my curiosity talking."

"Oh?" Goodnight said. "And how much trouble has *that* gotten you into before?"

"Tons," Clint said, rolling his eyes.

"And haven't you learned better by now?"

Clint hesitated a moment and then said, "Obviously not."

"Well," Goodnight said, "very few of us learn from our past mistakes, do we?"

"No," Clint said, "we don't."

# SIXTEEN

They made good time the next day, even with the wagonload of wire. As they came to within sight of Goodnight's spread, Clint stopped to take a look at it from a distance.

"It's very impressive," he said.

"Yes, it is," Goodnight agreed, "even from this distance. Wait until we get even closer, though. Then you'll really be impressed."

Goodnight was right. The closer they got, the more impressed Clint became. The house, when they finally reached it, was one of the largest he'd ever seen outside of a Southern plantation. The barn was the biggest he'd ever seen anywhere. The corral, in front of the barn, held some of the finest-looking horseflesh he'd ever laid eyes on.

As they rode up to the house, with Goodnight driving the wagon, they drew a crowd of ranch hands, one of whom stood out. He was a big man, standing about six four, with broad shoulders, a deep chest, and massive arms. He was blond and appeared to be in his early thirties. He was the one who spoke when they reached the house and the men who had grouped in front of it.

"Mr. Goodnight," the big man said. "We were starting to get worried. We expected you back yesterday."

"I know, Carl," Goodnight said, stepping down from the rig. "I ran into some trouble."

"Where are the others?" Carl asked. "Terry, and the rest?"

Clint had learned from Goodnight that Terry Lester was the man who had been injured during the first attempt on Goodnight's life, the man who had initially warned Clint away from the barbed wire.

"Terry was wounded, Carl, when somebody took some shots at me."

"Shots?" Carl said, looking and sounding concerned. "Are you all right, sir?"

"I am, thanks to this man," Goodnight said. "Uh, Carl, why don't you get the men back to work? Have someone take charge of this wagon and of my guest's horse."

"Yes, sir."

Carl turned and barked some orders at the men. Two of them stepped forward. One climbed atop the rig to drive it away, and the other man advanced on Clint and accepted Duke's reins.

"Take extra good care of that horse," Goodnight said.

"Yes, sir," the man said, and walked Duke away.

The other men dispersed, casting curious

glances back at Goodnight and at Clint. Obviously, they were wondering who he was.

"No reason for the other men to hear this yet, Carl," Goodnight said.

"Hear what, sir?"

"First, let me introduce the two of you," Goodnight said. "Carl Rivers, meet Clint Adams. He saved my life twice in Lubbock."

"Twice?" Carl asked.

"Clint," Goodnight said, "Carl is my foreman."

"Good to meet you," Clint said, and the two men shook hands briefly.

"Mr. Goodnight, you say he saved your life twice?" Carl said. "I don't understand. Where are the other men you took with you?"

"I want to talk to you about them, Carl," Goodnight said. "Let's go into my office, shall we? Clint? Would you come with us?"

"Of course."

Carl was looking at Clint and his boss with a bewildered look on his face.

"Come on, Carl," Goodnight said, putting his hand on his foreman's huge shoulder, "I'll tell you all about it inside."

In Goodnight's office Carl Rivers listened to his boss's story of the incidents that took place in and around Lubbock, and the part that Clint played in them. When Goodnight was done talking, Rivers was shaking his head.

"I can't believe it," the big man said. "I hired those men, Mr. Goodnight, all three of them. I can't believe that they all tried to kill you."

"Kill me or kidnap me, it really doesn't make much of a difference."

"When did you hire them, Carl?" Clint asked.

Carl looked at Clint, and then at his boss.

"Answer him, Carl."

"I'm not sure, really," the foreman said.

"Did you hire them all at the same time?"

"No," Carl said, "all three were hired separately. I don't even think they knew each other until they met working here."

"That could be," Clint said. "They could have been strangers and all been bought off separately."

"Or you're thinking that they could have been planted here one at a time," Goodnight said.

"I thought of that, yes."

"Which would mean that this thing was planned well in advance."

"Sessions," Carl said. "Do you think it was Frank Sessions, Mr. Goodnight?"

"Who's Sessions?" Clint asked.

"My nearest neighbor."

"Is he going to suffer the most from the wire you're going to put up?" Clint asked.

"Probably," Goodnight said. "We were sharing grazing land and water holes for a while, but he got too greedy. That's when I decided to fence it off."

"And he doesn't like it," Clint said.

"He hates it," Carl said. "And he especially hates barbed wire."

Clint looked at Goodnight and said, "Well, he sounds like a good number one suspect, Charles."

"Except for one thing," Goodnight said.

"What's that?"

"If Frank Sessions wanted me dead," Goodnight said, "he'd kill me himself. He's that kind of man."

"You seem fairly certain of that," Clint said.

"I am," Goodnight said.

"How?"

"I know him well," Goodnight said. "We used to be partners."

"What happened?"

"What usually happens to drive two men apart," Goodnight said.

"A woman?"

Goodnight nodded.

"We both fell in love with the same one."

"And?"

"And I married her," Goodnight said.

# SEVENTEEN

After Carl Rivers left, Goodnight told Clint to close the door of his office.

Just before Carl left, though, Goodnight reminded him to have someone go to Lubbock the next day to see about bringing Terry Lester back.

"I'll take care of it, sir."

The big man threw Clint an unreadable glance and left the room.

"How about a glass of sherry?" Goodnight asked, when Carl was gone.

"Sure, why not?"

Goodnight poured sherry into two crystal glasses from a similar decanter and handed one to Clint.

"After this I'll introduce you to my wife," he said, raising the glass. "I think you'll be as impressed with her as you were with the ranch."

"What about Rivers?" Clint asked.

"What about him?"

"Do you trust him?"

"He's my foreman."

"Yes," Clint said, "but do you trust him?"

There was the slightest hesitation before Goodnight said, "Yes."

"How long has he worked for you?"

"About six years," Goodnight said. "He's been foreman for two."

"Who was foreman before him?"

"A man named Harley Rose. Harley had been with me a long time."

"And what happened?"

"Somebody killed him."

"How?"

"A bar fight, over a woman, or a fifth ace, I believe," Goodnight said. "Maybe both. Harley was a gambler *and* a ladies' man."

"And then you made Rivers the foreman?"

"That's right," Goodnight said, "and he's done a fine job ever since. Are you saying that you suspect Carl of having something to do with this?"

"Well," Clint said, "he *did* hire the three men who tried to abduct you."

"He's hired a lot of men over the past two years, Clint."

Clint shrugged and said, "Hey, you know the man. If you trust him, then I suppose he's all right."

They finished the sherry, and Goodnight set aside the two glasses.

"Let's go and find my wife, Annie," Goodnight said. "After you've met her, I'll have you shown to your room so you can get cleaned up for dinner."

"Fine."

They left the office and Goodnight led Clint to a parlor. He'd expected the inside of the house to be lavishly, perhaps even outlandishly furnished, but instead it was done quite tastefully and in muted colors that, to Clint's way of thinking, did not fit Goodnight's personality.

"Don't think I had anything to do with it," Goodnight said, as if reading Clint's mind. "Annie bought all the furniture. If I had, there'd be a lot more overstuffed chairs in red and yellow. Have a seat, and I'll go and see where she is."

"All right."

Goodnight left the room, and Clint sat down rather than pace around. He thought a bit about Carl Rivers. If the other three men had been planted in advance, couldn't Carl Rivers also have been planted? No, that didn't make sense. Who would plant someone six years in advance? If you were going to start thinking that way, you'd have to suspect every man employed by Goodnight as being a possible plant. That was just too much to think about.

And so he decided not to.

He had finally taken to pacing, occasionally peering out the window, by the time Goodnight returned with his wife on his arm.

"Clint Adams," Goodnight said, making the introduction proudly, "this is my wife, Anne Goodnight."

Clint was stunned. Anne Goodnight was a statuesque redhead with clear, creamy skin and green eyes. As she smiled at him, he could have sworn that she was the same woman he had seen leaving

Goodnight's hotel room the morning they left, but he quickly realized that she was not. Although that woman had had similar hair and skin and had been of comparable age—perhaps late twenties—she was nowhere near as beautiful as this woman was.

It seemed that even when Goodnight cheated on his wife, he did so with look-alikes.

"Mr. Adams," she said, extending her hand.

He took it and found her handshake surprisingly firm—firmer than that of many men he had known.

"I have to thank you for saving Charles's life, not once but twice," she said. She released his hand and took hold of her husband's arm. "We're very grateful."

At a loss for words momentarily Clint finally said, "I was, uh, just glad to be able to help, Mrs. Goodnight."

"And I *am* so glad that you've consented to be our guest for a few days," she said. She turned to her husband and said, "Darling, I'm going to go and tell the cook to plan an extra special dinner."

"Dear," Goodnight said, "I'm sure Olivia has already started dinner—"

"Well, then," Anne Goodnight said, "she'll just have to start again. After all, how often do we have a very special guest such as Mr. Adams?"

"Please," Clint said, "don't go to any trouble."

"I'll go to as much trouble as I please, Mr. Adams," she said, with a smile that took away any sting her words might have had. "After all, it is my home, isn't it?"

"Yes, ma'am," Clint said, "that it is."

"Now, Charles," she said, "you make sure Mr. Adams is *very* comfortable, do you hear?"

"I hear you, dear," Goodnight said, "but since Clint *is* to be our guest for a while, I think it would be all right if you called him by his first name. Don't you think so, Clint?"

"Of course," Clint said, "I insist."

"Then you must call me Anne," she said.

"Or Annie," Goodnight said.

"Oh, darling," she said, "no one calls me Annie but you."

"Then I'll call you Anne," Clint said.

"That's fine," she said. "Now, if you gentlemen will excuse me? I'll see to dinner."

They both watched her leave the room, and then Goodnight turned to Clint.

"Well? Impressed?"

"Very," Clint said. "She's . . . lovely."

"She is much more than that," Goodnight said. He looked, for all intents and purposes, like a man head over heels in love with his wife.

Which made the incident with the woman leaving his hotel room even more puzzling.

"Come on then, Clint," Goodnight said. "I'll show you to your room myself."

# EIGHTEEN

Goodnight showed Clint to the second floor and his room, which was furnished in a similar fashion to the rest of the house that he had seen so far, tastefully, in muted colors.

"Make yourself comfortable," Goodnight told him. "I'll send someone up to get you when dinner is ready."

"I'd like to take a bath, if I can," Clint said.

"Of course. There's a tub in the room. I'll send someone up with water. Hot or cold?"

"Hot, please."

"I'll see to it."

"I'll also need my saddlebags—"

"And rifle," Goodnight said, cutting him off. "I'll see to it, Clint. Just make yourself comfortable."

Clint looked around the room and said, "I don't think I'll have a problem doing that."

"Good, good," his host said. "I'll see you for dinner, then."

Clint nodded. Goodnight backed out of the room

and closed the door. Clint turned, surveyed the room briefly, and then went to sit on the bed. The mattress was lush and, for most people, would have been extremely comfortable. Clint, however, was used to sleeping on the ground, or on mattresses that were no thicker than a folded blanket. In a bed like this he'd feel lost.

Of course, a mattress of this sort would be fine for lying with a woman. . . .

"Now that we've greeted our guest," Anne Goodnight said to her husband when he joined her in the kitchen, "tell me about what happened."

"I've told you already, dear," Goodnight said. "He saved my life twice."

"And once from your own men?" she asked, appalled. "How could that happen, Charles?"

"Annie, you never know if the men you hire are going to be dependable until you do hire them," Goodnight explained. "You know that."

"But to expect them to kill you? That's not something you can just accept. You had better talk to Carl Rivers about his hiring qualifications."

"I'll talk to him, Annie," Goodnight said, trying to soothe her. "Right now I have to see to our guest's needs. He wants a bath, and his belongings must be brought to him."

"You see to his belongings," Anne said, "and I'll see to his bath."

"But what about dinner—"

"I've already talked to Olivia about dinner," she replied. "I'll see that he gets his water."

"All right," Goodnight said. "He wants a hot bath, not a cold one."

"I'll see to it," she said, using a statement she had heard her husband use many times.

"All right," Goodnight said. "I'll send you a man to lug the water."

Anne Goodnight watched her husband leave the house by the back door, then turned and folded her hands in front of her face, as if in prayer, resting the tips of her fingers against her lips. She was thinking about Clint Adams sitting in a hot bath.

Clint was stripped to the waist, still wearing his jeans, when there was a knock at the door. Assuming that it was either a man with his belongings or a man with his hot water, he opened the door.

It was not a man, it was Anne Goodnight—*Mrs.* Charles Goodnight, he reminded himself as he took in her beauty once again.

"Oh," she said, eyeing his bare chest with obvious pleasure, "I'm sorry. I didn't mean to disturb you."

"You haven't," he said. "I'm waiting for my things, and some hot water."

"Yes, I know," she said, raising her eyes from his chest to his face. "Charles is seeing to your things, and I've arranged to have your water brought up. Did you locate the tub?"

"Uh, yes, I did—"

"It's over here," she said, boldly brushing past him into the room. She crossed the room to show him the tub, which stood behind a standing screen.

Deliberately leaving the door wide open—as wide as it could possibly go—Clint turned and faced her.

"Yes, Mrs. Goodnight," he said, "I managed to locate it myself."

"Oh," she said, folding her hands in front of her, waist high. "Of course. It wasn't hard to find, was it?"

"No, it wasn't."

She raised her eyebrows and said, "I thought we had established that you would call me Anne."

"Did we?"

"Yes, we did."

"Well," he said, "that was downstairs, not when we're alone in my room."

"Oh," she said, suddenly looking around her, "we are alone here, aren't we?"

"Yes, we are," Clint said. "If I may say so, I don't think it's proper."

"Well," she said, walking across the room toward him, "I'll leave then. I don't want to make you nervous. After all, you are our guest."

"Thank you for your concern," Clint said.

She went past him, and he noticed that she was a tall woman—and a sweet smelling one. She was wearing a green dress that went well with her red hair, but he found himself wondering what she'd look like in riding clothes, with a belt cinched tightly around her waist.

"The water will be here soon," she assured him. "I will see you at dinner."

"Thank you, Mrs.—uh, I mean, thanks, Anne."

She gave him a little wave and went out the door, which he closed after her—tightly. He was uncomfortable, not because he found her extremely attractive, but because he thought that she felt the same way about him. That was not the way to start up a new friendship, by sharing a mutual attraction with your new friend's wife.

# NINETEEN

Clint was fresh from the bath when there was a knock on his door. It was the fourth knock since his arrival. The first had been Anne Goodnight, followed closely by his belongings, and finally the water for his bath. He wrapped a towel around himself and hoped that he would be opening the door to Anne Goodnight again.

It was not his host's wife, however, but the man who had brought him his water.

"Mr. Goodnight says dinner will be served in fifteen minutes," the man said.

"All right," Clint said, aware that he was dripping on the floor, "thank you. I'll be there as soon as I dry off and dress."

He closed the door and proceeded to get ready for dinner.

When Clint came down for dinner, the Goodnights were already there. Charles Goodnight

was wearing a jacket and tie, making Clint feel
somewhat underdressed.

Anne Goodnight looked stunning. Once again
she was wearing green, but this time the dress was
low-cut, revealing creamy flesh and ample cleavage. She was a well-built woman, full-breasted,
broad-shouldered, and wasp-waisted.

"Sorry I didn't have something more fancy to
wear," Clint said as he sat.

"Don't worry about it," Goodnight said. "I hate
this dressing for dinner, but Annie insists on
it."

"It's the only civilized way to eat dinner," Anne
said.

Goodnight was seated at the head of the rec-
tangular table, and Anne Goodnight was sitting
right across from Clint. He found her cleavage
disconcerting, to say the least. Goodnight did not
seem to notice.

"I think you'll be very satisfied with dinner,"
Goodnight said. "It'll certainly be better than what
we had last night."

"Better than anything you've had in some time,
I hope," Anne Goodnight said. "Olivia is a wonderful cook."

Clint sniffed the air and said, "I'm sure it'll be
wonderful."

"How long do you think you'll be staying with
us, Clint?" Anne asked.

The question surprised him, especially since it
had come from her. Or perhaps it shouldn't have
surprised him. Not after her seemingly innocent
visit to his room.

"Oh, just for a few days I'm sure," Clint said. "No more."

"Well," Anne said, "maybe I'll have some company on an early morning ride while you're here. My husband is usually too busy to accompany me."

"You know I have to be up early, my dear," Goodnight said.

"So do I, darling," Anne said, "but not to work. What do you say, Clint? Would you ride with me in the morning? I understand from Charles that you have a beautiful horse. I'd love to see him."

"Well, I don't—"

"Oh, ride with her, Clint," Goodnight said, "or I might never hear the end of it."

He reached out and put his hand over his wife's, smiling at her.

"All right," Clint said. "I'd be happy to ride with you, Anne."

"Good!"

At that point a woman entered with a man behind her, bearing a tray of food. Clint assumed that the woman was the cook, Olivia. The man with the tray was the same man who had brought him his bathwater and then called him to dinner.

Clint watched as Olivia served dinner and noticed that the cook and the host's wife were not exactly on the best of terms. Clint wondered if that was simply because he was there and Anne Goodnight had invaded the kitchen, or if it was their usual relationship.

Speaking of relationships, all through dinner

Clint found himself wondering about the marriage of Charles and Anne Goodnight. They spoke to each other with affection but rarely seemed to touch. He had also been witness to a woman coming out of Goodnight's room at the hotel. Then there was the odd visit to his room by Anne Goodnight. Now the invitation for a morning ride, which may or may not have been an innocent one. Either way, the invitation was supported by her husband.

The dinner was delicious, as promised, but the rest of the situation was puzzling, to say the least.

# TWENTY

After dinner Goodnight invited Clint into his study for a glass of sherry. Anne Goodnight did not accompany them. In fact, Clint had no idea where she went after dinner, or whether or not he'd see her again. It was still early, and she had not yet bid him goodnight.

In the study Clint said, "The meal was wonderful."

"As I promised," Goodnight said, handing Clint a glass of sherry.

"And the spread is unbelievable."

"Well, you'll see more of it tomorrow when you go riding with Annie," Goodnight said. "By the way, I appreciate your agreeing to do that."

"No problem," Clint said. "I'd like to see some more of the place."

"Well, she'll show it to you," Goodnight said proudly. "She knows the place like the back of her hand, she's been back and forth over it so many times."

"She, uh, seems to be taking the news of the attempts on your life pretty well."

Goodnight's face sobered and he looked at Clint.

"Not as well as she would like us to believe, I'm afraid," Goodnight said. "She's quite frightened by it. That's another reason I'd rather not have her riding around alone."

Not afraid enough to go with her himself, Clint observed. He refrained from voicing his thought.

"You know," Goodnight said, "I wish you'd reconsider working for me."

"Charles—"

"I'd make you foreman, at a handsome salary," Goodnight added quickly.

"What about Rivers?"

"Well . . . Carl just might be in over his head in the job, Clint," Goodnight said.

"It's taken you two years to notice that?" Clint asked. "Or would you simply fire him in order to hire me?"

"Well, you have to admit," Goodnight said, "you would be the better man for the job."

"I doubt it," Clint said. "I've never ramrodded a major outfit, Charles. It's a little bit outside of my line of work."

"Well," Goodnight said, "take the next few days to think it over. I could use you here."

Clint thought that Goodnight was probably still thinking about him more as a gun than as a man. He could think all he wanted over the next few days, but Clint wasn't about to change his mind.

# TWENTY-ONE

After the sherry, Clint said he'd like to go outside for a walk.

"Feel free," Goodnight said. "You have the run of the place. I'd join you, but I have some paperwork to catch up on. I'll be in my office, though, if you want to talk about anything."

"All right," Clint said. "Thanks."

"Uh, do you always wear that?" Goodnight asked, indicating the gun on Clint's hip.

Clint looked down at it, and then back at his host.

"Sorry," Clint said. "Sometimes I forget that it's there."

"No problem," Goodnight said. "I can understand where a man of your . . . stature would have to wear it. It's okay, really."

"I *could* take it off while I'm here—"

"No, no," Goodnight said, holding up one hand. "I wouldn't think of asking you to do that, not if it would make you uncomfortable. Besides, I'd actually rather you did wear it, especially when you're around Annie. Forget I even brought it up. I was just . . . curious."

They left the study together and separated in the entry foyer. Goodnight went to the back of the house, where his office was, and Clint went out the front door.

It was brisk outside, but he decided not to go back inside for a jacket. He only intended to walk a bit, and when he got too cold he'd go back to the house.

Dinner had been a late affair, and it was already dark out. There were a few men roaming about, probably seeing to last minute chores, but for the most part he was alone, walking unnoticed.

Or so he thought.

When he reached the end of the house, furthest away from the barn and corral, he became aware that someone was standing there. He turned and saw Anne Goodnight. She was wearing a wrap, and her arms were crossed in front of her, as if she were trying to keep herself warm.

"Hello," she said.

"Anne," he said. "You shouldn't be out here."

"Why not?"

"It's cold."

"Is that the only reason?"

"What other reason would there be?"

She moved up alongside him and said, "Let's walk. You *were* taking a walk, weren't you?"

"Yes."

"Do you mind if I join you?"

"No, of course not."

They started walking, close together but not touching.

"Are you worried that someone might try to kill me, the way they did Charles?"

"Not really."

"It's a possibility, though, isn't it?" she asked. "That they might try to kill me, or abduct me? Perhaps to get at Charles?"

"Yes," he said, after a moment, "it is a possibility, Anne."

"I thought so," Anne said. "Charles is trying to tell me that it's not."

"Well, I don't want to contradict him—"

"You're not," she said. "He's trying to keep me from worrying. You're telling me the truth, which is the way I'd much rather have it."

They were getting further away from the house than he wanted to be with her. It was almost like being alone in his room.

"Anne," he said, stopping, "it's cold—"

She turned to face him and said, "You're afraid of me, aren't you?"

He stared back at her and said, "No."

She raised an eyebrow and said, "Wary, then?"

"Yes," he admitted, "wary."

"I won't bite you." She put her hand on his chest and said, "I feel safe with you around."

He stepped away, breaking the contact.

"What's wrong?"

"I just remembered something."

"What?"

"I had a dinner date with a woman in Lubbock two days ago."

It was true. He had just recalled asking Alicia Garfield to have dinner with him. In the wake of the second attempt on Charles Goodnight's life he had totally forgotten about it—until now.

"Oh?" she said. "With whom?"

"A woman named Alicia Garfield."

"Alicia," she said. "I think I know who she is. Dark-haired, works in the dress shop?"

"That's her."

"You know her?"

"Not really," he said, "and after this I doubt that I ever will."

"Pity," she said. "Well, shall we go back to the house?"

"Yes," Clint said gratefully, "yes, I think we should."

"Don't forget our date to ride tomorrow."

"I won't," he said. "How early?"

"Oh, I'm a *very* early riser," she said. "I'm usually up before the sun."

"Then I'll meet you at the barn at first light," he proposed.

"That would be fine."

When they reached the house they stopped and she turned to face him.

"Well, thank you for the walk, Clint . . . and the conversation."

"Don't mention it."

"I'll see you in the morning."

She started up the stairs, then turned and looked down at him.

"Aren't you coming in?"

"In a while," he said. "I just want to walk a bit more."

"Well, be careful," she said. "It's cold."

"I know," he said. But it was the oddest thing. As he watched her walk up the stairs to the front door and then enter, he didn't feel cold at all.

# TWENTY-TWO

The man standing in the barn watching Clint Adams had almost stepped from his cover to follow as Clint walked to the other end of the house. He stopped short when he saw a second figure join Clint, and then he recognized the second person as Mrs. Goodnight.

As Clint and Anne Goodnight walked away from the house, the darkness seemed to swallow them up. The man in the barn was sorely tempted to leave his cover and follow, but abruptly the two people stopped and walked back. He watched as they conversed in front of the house, and then Mrs. Goodnight went up the stairs and back inside.

Funny, he had only seen Clint Adams come out of the house. The woman must have come out from a door at the rear of the house.

Since the man's job was simply to watch, he did so as Clint started to walk, this time in the opposite direction. It was a few moments before the man realized that Clint Adams was now walking toward him!

The man panicked for a moment as he realized that Adams might be coming to the barn to check on his horse. He looked around, though, and realized that there were plenty of hiding places in the barn, if he needed them.

He was standing behind the barn doors now, peering out from a crack as Clint Adams continued to advance toward the barn. The man was just about to bolt from his present position to seek a hiding place when Clint changed direction and walked to the corral.

The man remained where he was, and watched.

Clint stopped at the corral. There were only a few animals left inside, and they were all fine-looking specimens. If these were any sample of the stock Goodnight was raising, then the man was very good at what he did.

One of the horses trotted over to where Clint was and nuzzled him.

"Looking for sugar?" Clint asked. "Sorry, I haven't got any." He pushed the animal's head and said, "Go on, go away."

Somebody on the ranch was probably in the habit of giving sugar to some of the horses, or maybe this particular one was a favorite. This was a young colt, probably not even broken yet. He watched as the animal trotted to the other side of the corral and stood with his back to Clint.

"Insulted?" Clint asked aloud. "Well, I'm sorry,

but I'm not in the habit of giving sugar to strange horses."

He turned away from the corral, briefly toyed with the idea of checking on Duke, then decided he could do that just as well in the morning. After all, he *was* meeting Anne Goodnight early—*very* early.

As he walked back to the house, he realized how tired he was. He'd been on the go virtually from the moment he'd first arrived in Lubbock—and his aim when he had arrived in town had been to rest.

He decided to make an early night of it.

From his position behind the barn door, the man watched Clint Adams walk back to the house, go up the steps, and enter. He came out of the barn and walked over to the corral. The same young colt who had nuzzled Clint for sugar came over and did the same to this man.

"Okay. Okay, boy," the man said, putting his hand in his pocket. "I've got your sugar for you."

# TWENTY-THREE

The next morning Clint rose before dawn, feeling refreshed. Turning in early the night before had been the right thing to do.

As he'd feared, though, he'd had to drag himself out of that comfortable bed. Sleeping in a bed like that night after night could get to be a habit—a bad habit.

He washed himself, using a basin and pitcher that were on a table near the now dry bathtub, then dressed and went downstairs. As far as he could see, there was no one moving about in the house. Maybe he had gotten up before Anne Goodnight.

He was about to leave when he did hear some sounds of activity from the kitchen. Probably the cook preparing to start breakfast. He thought about popping his head in, but if the woman resented Anne Goodnight invading her kitchen, how would she feel if *he* did it?

He went outside and walked toward the barn

instead. When he reached it, he heard someone moving around inside. As he went inside he saw Anne Goodnight, saddling a handsome bay mare.

"Good morning," he said.

She turned to face him, smiling.

"Well," she said, "you're up earlier than I thought. I barely beat you."

He had been right to wonder what she'd look like in riding clothes. She was wearing trousers and boots and a white shirt that looked like silk. The sleeves were big, even billowy. Her wide, shiny black belt made her waist seem even more impossibly slim than the night before. Her hair was down, hanging past her shoulders, and there was a green ribbon in it.

She looked incredible.

"I tried to saddle that beast of yours," she said, "but he wouldn't let me near him."

"He's like that sometimes," Clint said.

"He's beautiful, though, isn't he?"

"Don't let him hear you say that."

"Do you think he'd mind if I watched while *you* saddled him?"

"I think we can work that out," Clint said. "Come on."

"After all," she said, following Clint to Duke's stall, "you are the master, aren't you?"

"That's where you're wrong." They reached Duke's stall, and Clint reached out to touch the big gelding's huge head. "You see, neither of us is the master. We're partners."

"I see. Then he doesn't belong to you?"

Clint set about saddling Duke and said, "No, I

don't consider that I *own* him, not the way I own my . . . my gun, or my gun belt."

"You have an interesting relationship, then," she said while she watched.

"I suppose you could say that," Clint said. "We've saved each other's lives so many times that I've lost count. I don't even know who's up on who."

"I don't think it matters," she said. "Look how gentle he is while you saddle him. Are you the only one he trusts to let touch him?"

"Usually," Clint said.

"Fascinating."

Once Duke was saddled, Clint led him from the stall and over to where Anne's bay stood.

"This is Lindy," Anne said, stroking the white blaze on the mare's face. It extended from between the horse's eyes down to her nose.

"She's pretty."

Anne turned to look at him and said, "I notice you do what I do when you refer to horses."

"What's that?"

"Call them him or her rather than it, as Charles does."

"You don't like the way your husband does it?"

"No," she said, shaking her head, causing her hair to bounce nicely, "it's so cold and impersonal."

"Well, for your husband, horses are a business, Anne," Clint said. "It's understandable that he'd want to be impersonal where his business is concerned."

"I suppose so," she said. "He *is* good at what he does, isn't he?"

"So I understand," Clint said. "Shall we ride?"

"Yes," she said, her eyes sparkling. She obviously enjoyed riding. "Let's."

Not only did Anne Goodnight love to ride, but she loved speed. They galloped a bit until they were well away from the house, and then she suddenly kicked her heels into her horse's sides and off they went.

Clint urged Duke into a run, but kept the big gelding well within himself, allowing Anne to remain ahead of them. He knew he could have overtaken her anytime he wanted, but decided not to push Duke.

Eventually, she stopped and waited for him to catch up. When he did, he noticed that her color was high, she was breathing hard and—if possible—looked even more beautiful than ever. With a jolt he realized that she looked like she had just had sex—and wonderful sex, at that. He felt his own body responding to that.

"Do you think you could have caught me anytime?" she asked.

"Yes, I could have."

"Why didn't you?"

"I didn't think that was the point," he said, "for me to catch you. I thought we were just out riding."

"I like riding," she said, "but what I really want to do is race. I *love* speed."

"That's obvious."

She patted and rubbed the mare's neck and said, "She's the fastest horse on the ranch."

"She's pretty fast," he agreed.

She stared at him, eyes wide, and said, "I would love to race her against your horse."

Clint had raced Duke before, and the gelding had never been beaten. In fact, he had literally raced other horses into submission. Some of those animals had never been the same again. He would hate to see that happen to Anne's mare, Lindy.

"Uh, I don't usually race Duke."

"Why not?" she asked. "Afraid he'll be beaten?"

The sting he felt from her question was illogical—but it was there.

"He's never been beaten," Clint said, before he could stop himself.

"Well," she said, "there's always a first time. Want to race now?"

"No." He was angry with himself for allowing her to bait him.

"All right, 'fraidy cat," she said. "We'll just ride, then."

She started away, then turned in the saddle and shouted at him, "But I'll try not to run the poor old boy's legs off!"

She rode off laughing.

# TWENTY-FOUR

As Clint Adams and Anne Goodnight left the ranch for their morning ride, a man came out of the bunkhouse and saw them.

"Damn," he said, and started walking quickly toward the barn.

He actually wasn't sure what he was supposed to do. His job was to keep an eye on Goodnight and Clint Adams, but now Adams was riding off without Charles Goodnight. He was, however, with Goodnight's wife.

The man decided that Clint Adams took priority over Goodnight, simply because he was the man who had already saved Goodnight's life twice before. The man who was paying him didn't want Adams to be around for the third time.

He was almost to the front door of the barn when he heard someone call his name from behind. He turned and saw that it was the foreman, Carl Rivers.

"Where are you headin'?" Rivers asked.

"Just wanted to, uh, take a look at my horse, boss," the man said.

"Well, while you're looking at him, saddle him up," Rivers ordered.

The man asked, "Uh, am I goin' somewhere, boss?"

"Yeah," Rivers said, "you're goin' to Lubbock."

"What for?"

"To bring Terry Lester back," Rivers said, and then added, "that is, if he's in any shape to come back."

"Uh, that's a long ride, boss," the man said, trying to do something he just wasn't equipped to do—think fast.

"I know it," Rivers said. "That's why *you're* makin' it, and not me."

"Uh-huh," the man said.

"Well . . . get to it!" Rivers said. "I want you back here in three days, tops."

"I hear you," the man said.

He turned and walked to the barn. He had two employers, Charles Goodnight and the man who had hired him to keep an eye on Goodnight and Adams. It would take him the length of time it took him to saddle his horse to decide which of his employers' instructions it would be wisest to follow.

# TWENTY-FIVE

"Do you know what I'd like to see?" Clint said to Anne Goodnight.

"What?"

The look she gave him was a bold one, and he thought he knew what she was thinking. It wasn't something a married woman should have on her mind, either—unless it was with her husband. Of course, he could have been wrong. . . .

"The wire."

"What?"

"I'd like to see some of the barbed wire that's already up."

"For God's sake, why?" she asked.

"I've never seen it," he said. "I saw it all coiled up in the back of your husband's wagon. I think I'd like to see it strung."

"It's disgusting!" she said.

"You don't approve?"

"I don't . . . but that's my husband's business."

"You haven't told him of your disapproval?" he asked her.

"No," she said, shaking her head. "He never asks me about his business, and I don't butt in. It's the way he wants it."

"Look," he said, "if you don't want to—"

"No, no," she said, tossing her hair over her shoulder, "if you want to see it, I'll show it to you. We're not far from a stretch of it now. I was going to turn back, but we'll go on ahead."

"Anne—"

"Come on," she said. "It's not far."

She rode off and he followed. Had he known how much she disliked the wire he wouldn't have asked, but now that he had he was looking forward to having his curiosity satisfied.

"There it is." she said.

They had just topped a rise and she was pointing downhill. He looked ahead of them and saw that the wire was strung out as far as he could see in both directions.

"Whose land is on the other side?" he asked.

"That's part of the Sessions spread," she said. "Frank Sessions."

"I understand he and your husband were once friends," Clint said.

"Yes," she said, and then looked at him and added, "and I suspect you know why they are no longer friends, don't you?"

"It had something to do with you, I believe," he said. It was another subject—like the wire—that he now wished he hadn't brought up. "I'm sorry," he said, "I spoke without thinking."

"It's all right," she said, looking down at the wire. "Not talking about it is not going to make it go away, is it? They both fell in love with me, and it made enemies out of two men who were once friends." She looked at him and added, "I'm not proud of it, you know."

"I don't think it's your fault," he said. "You shouldn't feel proud or ashamed."

"Oh," she said, "I don't feel ashamed. I didn't say that. I just said I wasn't proud of it. Truthfully, I think they were both silly about the whole thing."

She looked away from him, back at the wire, and said, "Well, there it is. Why don't you go down and take a look at it? I'll wait here."

He was going to protest, but finally said, "All right." He really did want to see it up close. "I won't be long."

She looked away from him and the wire and said, "Take as long as you like."

He stared at her for a moment, but when she kept her face averted he urged Duke on down the hill toward the wire.

About a mile on the other side of the wire Sam McCallum, the foreman of the Sessions ranch, and several of his men were attempting to round up some stray cattle.

"How many we got?" McCallum asked a man named Harvey Dunn.

"About a dozen, boss."

"There should be a few more," McCallum said. "Why don't you and the men take these back. I'll scout up ahead and see what I can find."

"Why not take a man with you?" Dunn asked. "I don't need all the men to take these strays back."

"Okay," McCallum said. "Tell Webster to ride with me, and the rest of you head back."

"Okay, boss," Dunn said.

As Dunn went to tell Webster, McCallum looked off in the distance. He knew he was about a mile away from Charles Goodnight's wire, and he had a strange feeling of dread about it.

God, he hated that wire!

Clint rode Duke up to the wire and stared down at it without dismounting. It looked benign enough to him. Of course, you could see what damage it *might* do under the proper circumstances, but just *being* there the way it was, it seemed more a deterrent than something . . . malevolent. It did not seem to him something that someone should kill over.

He dismounted to touch it, rather than ride Duke too close to it.

"Stand easy, big boy," he said as he released Duke's reins and walked up to the wire.

He looked up at Anne once, but she was still not looking his way.

He walked to the wire then and touched it. He could see that it was strung very tautly, and the points of the wire were very sharp. In fact, had he not been extra careful he might have actually cut his finger.

He turned and looked up at Anne once again, and found it odd that she was not there. He looked right and then left and saw her riding away at a fast gallop. Had she succumbed to some basic fear of the wire and decided to run away from it? No, as he watched he became positive that she was not running *away* so much as she was running *to* something.

He did not know what she had seen, but whatever it was, it had been enough to make her rush to it.

He mounted Duke, swung him around, and started after her.

# TWENTY-SIX

Anne heard him coming and turned to look at him. Her eyes were streaming with tears, and her hands were covered with blood.

"Help him!" she cried.

She still had her hands on the bleating—and *bleeding*—calf, who had somehow gotten himself tangled up in the barbed wire. This, then, was what she had seen that had sent her off in such a rush.

Clint dismounted and went to her side. It was then that he saw that all of the blood was not the calf's. In fact, she had cut her hands on the wire in her attempt to free the helpless animal.

"All right," he said, taking her wrists and firmly pulling her hands away, "let me do it. You're just making your own cuts worse."

She allowed him to pull her hands away, and then he went back to look the situation over while she tried to calm the calf. The more the poor beast struggled, the worse the situation got.

"If I had something to cut the wire with—" he said.

"Oh, do something, Clint! Please! He'll die if we don't get him out."

It was true. If the calf kept struggling, the bleeding would get worse and he would die.

"All right," he said, "there's only one thing I can see to do."

He drew his gun. Anne's eyes went wide.

"No!" she shouted.

"I'm not—" he started, but he was cut short by the sound of a shot.

"Holster your gun, mister," a voice said. "You ain't shootin' that calf."

Both Clint and Anne looked at the two men who were sitting their horses on the other side of the fence.

"Mr. McCallum," Anne said, "we're trying to get this animal free. Is he one of yours?"

"Yes, ma'am," McCallum said, "and I can't see how you can help it by killin' it."

"I'm not planning on killing him," Clint said.

"Then why the gun?"

"I can't untangle him from the wire if I can't cut it," Clint said. "Do you have something to cut it with?"

"No," McCallum said.

"Then let me do it my way, before he bleeds to death," Clint said.

McCallum still wasn't sure what Clint had in mind, obviously, but he holstered his own gun—and waved his man to do the same. Then he said, "Go ahead, mister."

"I'll need your help, since you're here," Clint said.

"Why should I help you?"

"It's your calf, isn't it?" Clint asked. "Besides, Mrs. Goodnight isn't strong enough for what I want."

The two men exchanged glances, and then McCallum nodded and they both dismounted.

"What do you want us to do?" McCallum asked, as they both approached the fence.

"Hold on to the animal," Clint said. "When I fire he might try to bolt, and he'll cut himself even worse."

The two men exchanged glances again, then crouched by the animal and took hold of him.

There were three strands of wire. Clint held the barrel of his gun to the first strand and fired. The bullet severed it cleanly. The calf cried out and tried to bolt, but the two men held him fast.

Anne Goodnight and Sam McCallum finally realized what Clint's intention had been with the gun. Against his better judgment, McCallum felt admiration for the man's ingenuity. Anne Goodnight simply felt foolish that she had misinterpreted his intention.

Clint fired twice more, and when the three strands were cut, he and the other men were able to unwind the wire from the calf and free him.

Clint, Anne, and McCallum watched while the other man examined the calf's wounds.

"How bad, Webster?" McCallum asked.

"Could've been worse, boss," Webster said. "We treat his cuts, he should be all right."

"Good," McCallum said. He looked at Clint, and then at Anne. "We're obliged for your help, but the fact remains, Mrs. Goodnight, that your husband's wire is responsible for this."

"Mr. McCallum," Anne said archly, "if you could control your cattle, this would not have happened."

McCallum gave her a calm look and said, "Strays are strays, ma'am. It happens."

McCallum looked at Clint and said, "What's your name, mister?"

"Clint Adams."

"Mine's McCallum," the man said, "Sam McCallum. I'm the ramrod of the Sessions outfit. That was pretty smart what you did. I'm sorry I drew down on you."

"That's all right," Clint said. "You had no way of knowing what I was planning."

While he spoke, Clint ejected the spent shells from his gun and replaced them with live ones. McCallum watched every move.

"Well, we better get this calf back to the ranch and treat his cuts. Again, much obliged for your help."

McCallum put his hand out and Clint shook it briefly. The Sessions foreman tipped his hat to Anne, and then he mounted his horse. The other man, Webster, lifted the calf and handed him up to McCallum, who draped him over his saddle in front of him. He was unmindful of the blood he was getting on his hands and clothes.

Webster mounted up, and the two men rode away.

Clint turned and looked at Anne, who also had blood on her clothes and hands, some of it hers.

"Let me see your hands."

"They're all right," she said, but she couldn't seem to close them.

"Is there any water nearby?"

"There's a water hole. . . . It's about half a mile away," she said.

"Let's get over there and wash those cuts, and then I'll bind them."

"It can wait—"

"No, it can't," Clint said. "Come on."

He helped her into her saddle, then mounted Duke and took hold of her reins. She kept her arms folded in front of her, her hands palms up, while he led her horse to the water hole.

# TWENTY-SEVEN

When they reached the water hole Clint helped Anne down from her horse and sat her down on the ground at the water's edge. He then pulled his shirt out of his pants and tore three strips from it.

"Put your hands in the water," he said.

She did so.

"It hurts," she said, "and it's cold."

"Good," he said.

He took one hand out of the water, leaving the other in. Using one of the strips he'd torn from his shirt, he tried to clean the wounds. She had three cuts in the palm of this, her right hand. Two seemed superficial, but one, right in the center of her palm, seemed fairly deep. Once he had it cleaned as well as he could, he bound it, making sure that he did so tightly, to staunch the flow of blood from the bad cut.

"Give me your other hand."

She did, and he examined it and cleaned it.

This one had four cuts in it, but none of them were serious.

"You knew those men?" he asked while he worked.

"Only McCallum, because he's Frank Sessions's foreman. The other man was just a hand."

"How does your husband get along with McCallum?" Clint asked.

"He doesn't deal with him."

"What about Rivers?"

"What about him?"

"Does he know McCallum?"

"I'm sure he does," she said, "but I have no idea how well."

He bandaged the hand less tightly than he had the other. She was able to flex the left hand, but not the right.

"Can you ride?" he asked.

"I can direct the horse with my knees, if need be," she said. "I'm an excellent rider."

"I know you are."

She stared at him and then said, "I'm sorry. I'm being too sensitive. Thank you for taking care of my hands—and for freeing that calf."

"Well . . . you were obviously distressed about it," he said. "I had to do something."

"Are your hands cut?" she asked.

"Not badly," he said, and showed her. He had a cut on each hand, but they were both superficial.

"I'm sorry," she said.

She took his right hand in hers so she could look at it, then brought it closer to her face. Before he knew what she was doing, she had pressed her mouth to it. He felt almost helpless as she ran her tongue over the cut.

"Anne—"

She looked at him, then got to her knees, leaned close to him, and kissed his mouth. For a moment he responded, opening his mouth so that her tongue had free entry into it. Abruptly, though, he took her by the shoulders and pushed her away without releasing her.

"This isn't right," he said.

"I know," she said, but her eyes were shining. He could see that although she agreed with him, she really didn't care whether it was right or wrong.

He released her shoulders and stood up.

"We should get back and tell Charles what happened," he said.

She smiled and got to her feet.

"Everything that happened?" she asked.

He frowned at her, then turned and mounted Duke, leaving her to mount up on her own. As he watched her climb atop her horse without much difficulty, he thought that he could still feel her tongue on his hand, and her kiss on his lips.

Maybe it was time for him to leave the Goodnight ranch.

# TWENTY-EIGHT

When they got back to the ranch, Goodnight was still out with some of his men.

"You'd better go inside and wash those hands again," Clint said, as they both dismounted. "I'll take care of the horses."

"Come up to the house when you're finished," she said. "We can have something to drink."

"Anne—"

"And talk."

He frowned, but said, "All right."

"Maybe my husband will be back by then."

He watched as she turned and walked toward the house, and hoped that Charles would indeed be home when he got there.

He knocked on the front door, and when there was no answer he tried the doorknob and found the door unlocked. Against his better judgment, he opened the door and went inside.

"Anne?" he called.

There was no answer.

"Charles?"

When there was still no answer, he went into the dining room and through to the kitchen. He opened the kitchen door and stuck his head in. The cook, Olivia, turned her head and glared at him. She was a big woman, with powerful-looking arms. He didn't think he'd ever want to be the object of her anger.

"Yes?"

"I'm sorry," he said. "I was looking for Mrs. Goodnight."

"Well, she ain't in here," the cook said, with obvious approval.

"I, uh, see that," he said. "I'll, uh, I'll just look elsewhere."

"Fine."

He backed away and let the door close. When he turned, he saw Anne Goodnight standing there looking at him.

"She doesn't like people in her kitchen, does she?" he asked.

"You noticed that?"

He looked at her hands and saw that she had put proper bandages on them.

"How are your hands?"

She looked down at them briefly and then said, "They're fine."

"That's good."

They stared at each other awkwardly for a while. She had changed from her riding clothes into a simple dress in solid blue. It buttoned all the way up to her neck.

"Come along with me," she said, "and we'll have something to drink. Charles is not home, yet, and may not be for some time."

He was following her from the dining room through the entry foyer when there was a knock on the door. They stopped, and he watched as she went to the door. When she opened it, Carl Rivers stepped in.

"Mrs. Goodnight," he said, respectfully removing his hat.

"Carl."

He looked down at her hands, at Clint, and then at Anne's face.

"One of the boys told me he saw you and Mr. Adams ride in," Rivers said. "Said something looked funny. What happened to your hands?"

"There was an accident," she said, putting her hands behind her, out of sight, as if she had done something wrong and was trying to hide them. "With the wire."

"The wire?" Rivers asked, frowning.

"A calf was caught up in the wire," Clint said. "Mrs. Goodnight tried to free it without my help."

"I see," Rivers said. He did not look at Clint, but chose to continue staring at Anne Goodnight. Clint had the feeling that there might be more going on here between the two of them than immediately met the eye. "Whose calf was it?"

"It was a Sessions calf."

Rivers nodded.

"Two men happened by while we were trying to free it," Clint offered. "Their names were, uh, Webster, and Sam McCallum."

"McCallum," Rivers said. Now he looked at Clint. "Was there any trouble with them?"

"No," Clint said, "no trouble. In fact, they helped us free the calf, and then took it with them."

"I see," Rivers said. To Anne Goodnight he said, "Do you need a doctor?"

She started to say, "No—" but Clint interrupted and said, "It wouldn't be a bad idea. Do you have to send to town for him?"

"There's one in town," Rivers said, "but old Doc Handley lives near here. He used to be the town doctor until he retired."

"Will he come?" Clint asked.

Rivers looked directly into Clint's eyes and said, "I'll send someone to get him."

"Send someone to *ask* him to come, Carl," Anne Goodnight said firmly.

Rivers looked at Anne Goodnight and said, "Yes, ma'am. As you say. I'll take care of it."

Now there was an awkward moment there among all three of them before Rivers nodded, put his hat on, and left the house.

Anne turned and looked at Clint.

"I really don't need a doctor."

He smiled at her and replied, "Just as I said, it wouldn't be a bad idea."

She still had her hands behind her back when she said, "Come on, I think I need a drink."

# TWENTY-NINE

They went into the parlor where Clint had first
met Anne, and she walked over to a sideboard to
pour some brandy.

"Want some?" she asked Clint.

"Too early for me," he told her. "You go ahead."

"For the pain," she said. "Please sit."

He sat at one end of the sofa, and she chose to
sit at the other, with a single cushion between
them. She held the glass in her less injured hand.

"I'm sorry," Clint said suddenly, "but I notice
some things going on here."

She lifted her chin and asked, "Like what?"

"Like . . . what was going on between you and
Carl Rivers just now?"

She elevated her chin just a fraction higher and
asked, "What do you mean?"

"I think you know what I mean, Anne."

She hesitated a few moments, killing the time
sipping her brandy, and then she said, "Nothing's
going on . . . now."

"But there was, at one time, wasn't there?"

"Yes."

Now he waited, watching her to see if she would continue.

She used her free hand to smooth her dress in her lap, and then looked at him.

"My husband . . . works very hard, Clint. He has to, in order to build the kind of empire he wants. I admire him for that."

He remained silent.

"It does, however, leave me alone quite a bit," she said. "We're not—he is a very sweet man, really . . . but Charles is not the most . . . romantic . . . of men . . ."

He saw how much difficulty she was having with this and decided to take pity.

"Look, Anne," he said, interrupting her, "I'm sorry, I was out of line—"

"No, no," she said. "You deserve to know. I mean, I don't want you to think that I'm a . . . tramp, or anything—"

"I don't think that."

"There have been other men, Clint," she said, "at other times. . . . Nothing very serious, you understand . . . and my husband knows nothing about . . . about any of them. . . ."

"How serious was it with Rivers?"

She compressed her lips and said, "Not very serious . . . on my part . . . and with Carl it was . . . a mistake."

"How long . . . uh, how long ago was—"

"Carl?" she said. "It's been over four months."

"It must be difficult. . . ."

"More so for him, I fear," she said. "I told him in the beginning that there could be nothing . . . serious, nothing *permanent* between us. He said he understood . . . and yet . . ."

"He fell in love with you."

She nodded.

"I suspect that many men fall in love with you, Anne," he said. "Your husband, Frank Sessions, Carl Rivers . . ."

She looked at him boldly and asked, "And you?"

"No," he said, shaking his head, "not me. I don't make it a habit of falling in love with other men's wives."

"I see," she said, lowering her eyes now. "That's probably . . . wise."

"Of course," he added, "I haven't known you that long. . . ."

She looked up at him then and smiled, and he could see how men fell in love with her. There was something between them, even now. Not love, certainly not that, but an attraction was undeniable. It had been so ever since they first met, and Clint could not understand how Charles Goodnight could not see it. He also could not understand how a man could neglect a wife like Anne Goodnight.

It caused them both to start when they suddenly heard the front door close. Neither of them had heard it open.

Abruptly, Charles Goodnight came striding into the room.

"Ah, good, you're both here," he said. He was slipping a pair of black leather gloves from his hands. Clint wondered if he just liked the way they looked, or if they were necessary for handling the wire. "We were stringing some wire in Parson's Meadow when we ran into Sam McCallum and some of his men."

Goodnight went immediately to his wife's side and fell down on one knee. He took her free hand in his.

"McCallum told me what happened with the calf, and the wire. Are you all right?"

"I'm fine, Charles."

Goodnight looked at Clint, who said, "Rivers is sending for Doc Handley."

"Doc Handley," Goodnight said. "All right, that's good, that's very good."

"Did anything happen between you and McCallum's men?" Anne asked.

"We were stringing the wire and some of McCallum's men rode up. It was fairly tense, and I thought that something would happen, but then McCallum came along. The man has a cool head, I'll say that for him. He kept anything from occurring."

"I had the impression he was . . . formidable," Clint said.

"He is," Goodnight said. "He worked for me once."

"Really?"

"Yes," Goodnight said, "before he left to work for Frank Sessions."

"I see."

"Dear," Anne said to Goodnight, "why don't you go and wash up? Clint and I will wait here."

"Actually," Clint said, putting his glass aside and standing up, "I'd like to get cleaned up myself."

"Of course," Anne said.

Goodnight fronted Clint and said, "McCallum told me how you handled the wire."

Clint braced himself, thinking that maybe Goodnight was going to take him to task for severing the wire.

"It was smart," Goodnight said instead, "very good thinking."

"Thank you."

"Of course," he said, "I've sent some men out there to restring it."

"Of course," Anne said.

"Well," Goodnight said, "perhaps I will clean up, then."

"I'll wait here," Anne said to both of them. "Doc Handley should be here shortly."

"I'll be back before he arrives," Goodnight said. He leaned over and kissed his wife's cheek. "I'm glad you're all right."

"I'm fine," she said. "Clint kept me from being too badly cut."

Goodnight looked at Clint and said, "Then that puts me further in your debt, sir."

Clint would have protested, but he knew it would do no good. He simply nodded, and both men left Anne Goodnight there to go and get cleaned up.

On the way up to his room Clint thought back to their meeting with Sam McCallum. At the time he had not noticed anything going on between

Anne Goodnight and McCallum, but then he *had* been fairly preoccupied. Now he found himself wondering if McCallum was one of those many men who had fallen in love with her.

# THIRTY

When Clint came back down, his own cut hand cleaned, his clothes fresh, there was a white-haired man in the parlor with Charles and Anne Goodnight. As he entered, he saw that the man was sitting next to Anne on the sofa, ministering to her injured hands. There was a glass of whiskey close at hand. Clint wondered why so many doctors he had known drank so much. Was it because they dealt so much with other people's pain?

"Ah, there you are, Clint," Goodnight said. He was standing by, watching the doctor work. "This is Doc Handley. Doc, this is Clint Adams."

Handley did not look away from his work.

"Good to meet you, Mr. Adams," the doctor said. "I've heard a lot about you."

Clint couldn't be sure if the doctor was talking about his reputation in general, or simply that he'd heard about him from the Goodnights.

"I understand," the man went on, bandaging

Anne's hands, "that your own hands were injured by the wire, as well?"

"Not really," Clint said. "A few minor cuts, is all. Nothing to concern yourself about."

"Well," Handley said, "my guess is you been cut or injured a time or two before, so you must know what you're talkin' about."

"I do."

"Fine, then," Handley said. He finished Anne's hand, then reached for his whiskey.

"Done, Doc?" Goodnight asked.

"I've done all I can," Handley said after a healthy swallow of whiskey. "They'll heal just fine. Cleanin' 'em up right away was a good idea."

"That was Clint's—Mr. Adams's idea," Anne said. "He insisted."

"Good thing he did, too," Doc Handley said. "Kept any chance of infection to a minimum."

Handley finally looked up at Clint, and Clint was surprised to see that the old man had to be in his eighties, at least. His face was so heavily lined it looked like some sort of map. His eyes were blue, liquid, almost faded, and yet they betrayed the fact that the mind behind them was still sharp.

"That damned wire . . ." Doc Handley said to no one in particular.

"Come on, Doc," Goodnight said, "I'll have someone take you back home. What do I owe you?"

Handley, staring into his glass, said, "A bottle of this fine whiskey would do nicely."

"You've got it," Goodnight said.

He assisted the doctor to his feet, and they walked from the room together.

"How do your hands feel?" Clint asked Anne.

"They're fine," she said. "Time for everyone to stop making such a fuss over me."

"If that's what you want."

She looked up at him then and smiled.

"Oh, what woman really wants that, right?" she asked him.

"None that I've known," he said. "Women like being fussed over, don't they?"

"I'll bet you know that for a fact," she said to him. "I bet you've known a lot of women, Clint Adams."

"A few."

"Was there ever someone . . . special?"

"There was . . . once."

"Once?"

He gave her a wan smile and said, "She died."

"I'm sorry," she said. "And now?"

"Now?" he said. He thought briefly of the ladies he'd known. He shook his head and said, "No. No one special."

"You travel quite a bit, I bet."

"Yes."

"Why is that?"

He shrugged.

"I guess I just never found one place I'd like to stay in forever."

"Do you think you ever will?"

"I don't know," he said. "No, that's not true. The answer is no. I don't honestly think there is a place out there like that for me."

"Really?" she said. She was silent for a moment, and then she said, "I think that's sad."

He thought about it for a moment as well, wondering if he thought so, too.

# THIRTY-ONE

If Charles Goodnight noticed any awkwardness between Clint and his wife, Anne, he certainly didn't show it at dinner. He talked away about the length of wire they had strung that day, and how much they would be stringing the following day and the rest of the week.

"Before long," he said, "I'll have every foot of my property fenced and wired, and then let the bastards complain."

"Do you have that much wire, dear?" Anne asked, with something less than real interest.

"Not yet," Goodnight said, "but I will, soon."

"Charles," Anne said, "what do you intend to do about the attempts on your life?"

"What can I do?"

"You can find out who it was."

"Who it was?" Goodnight repeated. "I know who it was, Annie."

"You do?" she asked.

"Well," he said, hedging, "I have a pretty good idea, don't I?"

"You mean . . . Frank Sessions?"

"Who else?"

"You do have other neighbors who object to the wire, Charles," she pointed out.

"No one who objects as much as Sessions does," he told her.

"And then there are the people who simply don't like the wire."

Goodnight shook his head.

"There is no one who is as against it as Frank Sessions is."

Anne looked across the table at Clint, probably for support, but since Clint did not know Frank Sessions at all, there was nothing he felt he had to offer.

"Well, then," she finally said, "if you're so sure, why don't you do something about it?"

Goodnight gave Clint an amused look, as if to say "Isn't she cute?" and then looked at his wife.

"What would you suggest, dear?"

"Go and talk to him."

"To Sessions?"

"Of course, to Sessions."

"About what?"

"About the attempts on your life!" she said, exasperated.

"Why should I talk to him about the attempts on my life?" Goodnight asked. "He *knows* about them. He was *behind* them."

Once again Anne looked across the table at

Clint, imploring him to say something.

"This doesn't sound like a bad idea, Charles," Clint said.

The look on Anne's face clearly said, "Thank you!"

"What?" Goodnight said, looking at him. "What are you saying, that you agree with her?"

"Sure," Clint said. "Why not talk to Sessions? Are you a hundred percent sure he was behind the attempts on your life?"

"Well . . . no," Goodnight said, backing off a step now that Clint had taken up Anne's cause, "I'm not one *hundred* percent sure—"

"Then why not go and talk to the man and find out?" Clint said.

"You mean . . . just ask him?" Goodnight asked incredulously.

"No, you don't have to come right out and ask him," Clint said, "but you can talk to him, and watch his face, and be able to tell if he was behind any of it."

Goodnight looked at his wife, who nodded to him and then back at Clint.

"Let me get this straight," Goodnight finally said. "You've done this before? Looked into a man's face and been able to tell if what he was saying was the truth?"

"I have."

Goodnight hesitated, then exploded.

"Excellent!" he said, with enthusiasm.

"Then you'll do it?" Anne asked.

"Of course I will, dear," he said, "if it will put your mind at ease."

She smiled and said, "Oh, it would, Charles."

"Fine, then," he said, patting her hand. He looked at Clint and said, "We'll leave for the Sessions ranch first thing in the morning."

"What?" Clint said. "What do you mean, *we*?"

"Well, you're coming with me, naturally," Charles said. "Otherwise, how am I going to tell if he's telling the truth or lying?"

"I just told you—"

"You told me that *you* can tell by looking at a man," Goodnight said. "*I* don't have that ability, Clint, you do. So, I'll need you to come with me."

"Charles—"

"Please, Clint," Anne said, cutting him off. "Go with him and keep him out of trouble."

Goodnight beamed at his wife, then looked at Clint and asked, "How can you turn down a face like that?"

Clint stared across the table into Anne Goodnight's face—her lovely face—and he knew that he was being manipulated.

"All right."

"You'll do it?" she asked.

"Yes," he said sourly.

"Excellent!" Goodnight said again.

"But tell me something, Charles," Clint said, looking at his host.

"What?"

"If it isn't Sessions who was behind the attempts, what will you do then?"

"That's easy," Goodnight said. "We can go and talk to all of my neighbors, and you can pick out the guilty man for me."

"Now wait—"

"I don't know how to thank you for your help, Clint," Anne said.

"Listen," Clint said, "the two of you have gotten the wrong idea—"

"I'm kidding, Clint," Goodnight said. "If you think Sessions is not my man, then maybe Frank himself will have some ideas about who is."

"You'd work with Sessions?" Clint asked.

"Hey, if he would work with me, why not?" Goodnight said, and then added, "But I mean on this. I don't mean that we'd become partners again."

"Of course not," Clint said.

"So whether he did it or not, we'll deal with that when the time comes. Agreed?"

Clint looked at Charles Goodnight, then back to Anne's eager face, and finally said, "All right, agreed."

# THIRTY-TWO

"Okay, tell me again, what happened?" Frank Sessions said.

Sam McCallum was standing in front of Sessions on the porch of the man's house. He had just finished relating to him all of the occurrences of the day. It was what they usually did at this time of the evening, the foreman reporting to the employer.

Only this time, there was more interesting news than usual.

McCallum took a deep breath and then told Sessions again about the calf, Anne Goodnight and Clint Adams, and then about interrupting what was about to become a battle between Goodnight and his men and Sessions's men.

"Are you sure the man said his name was Clint Adams?" Sessions asked.

"Positive, boss," McCallum said. "He told me his name was Clint Adams."

"The Gunsmith."

"He didn't say that."

"He didn't have to," Sessions said. He was a tall man, taller than McCallum, but not as young and not as well-built. "If he said his name was Clint Adams, then he's the Gunsmith."

"That's what I figured."

"You know what that means, don't you?" Sessions asked his foreman.

"What?"

"Goodnight has gone and hired himself a gun," Sessions said.

McCallum frowned and said, "That wasn't the impression I got."

"What makes you say that?"

"Oh, the man's actions," McCallum said. "If he was a hired gun, I think he might have tried to take the two of us."

"Well, you're lucky he *didn't* try, because he probably would have succeeded."

"You think so?" McCallum asked, with a wounded look.

"Come on, Sam," Sessions said. "You're not a gunman, and you know it."

Grudgingly, McCallum said, "Well, maybe not, but I'm no slouch."

"Besides, you don't get paid enough to go up against a man like the Gunsmith," Sessions said, "and neither does anyone else around here."

"That's true enough."

"So," Sessions said, rubbing his long jaw, "maybe what we need around here is someone who does."

"You mean . . . hire your own gunman?"

"Why not?" Sessions said. "Goodnight's opened the door now, hasn't he? If this erupts into some kind of a range war, it will be his doing, won't it?"

Shaking his head, McCallum said, "I told you before, boss, I don't think Adams is here as a gunman."

"What other reason could he have for being here?" Sessions asked.

"Well . . . he was with Mrs. Goodnight, maybe Goodnight hired him as her bodyguard."

That stopped Sessions for a moment.

"Why would she need a bodyguard?"

"Well, somebody tried to kill Goodnight—twice! Maybe he's worried about his wife."

"Maybe," Sessions said, rubbing his jaw again.

"Maybe what we—uh, you should do is try to find out what Adams *is* doing here."

"And how would you suggest I do that?"

McCallum shrugged and then said, "Ask him?"

# THIRTY-THREE

Early the next morning Clint came down for breakfast and found Charles Goodnight waiting for him.

"Thought I was going to have to come up and wake you," Goodnight said amiably.

"I'm not a rancher," Clint said, "so I don't rise as early as you do."

"That's okay," Goodnight said. "I've got Olivia making some eggs for us, and then we can get started."

"Get started?"

"Have some coffee," Goodnight said, indicating a pot that was already on the table.

"Thanks."

As Clint poured himself a cup, Goodnight said, "Yes, we have to go see Frank Sessions, remember? You're going to read his mind."

Clint sat down with his coffee and shook his head slowly.

"I tried to tell you and Anne last night that you

had the wrong idea about what I was saying,"
Clint tried to explain.

"That's all right," Goodnight said. "It's a sound
idea anyway, to go and talk to him. In fact, I know
Frank pretty well; I'll probably know if he's lying
or not."

"Doesn't Anne usually have sound ideas?" Clint
asked him.

"She's a smart girl," Goodnight said, "but she
doesn't usually get involved in my business."

"Maybe she should."

Goodnight gave him a look.

"She's a woman," he said, as if that explained
it all away.

Clint opened his mouth to speak, but at that
moment Olivia came in from the kitchen bearing
a big plate of bacon and eggs.

"I'll bring out the biscuits," she said.

"Does she ever smile?" Clint asked, when she'd
left.

"No," Goodnight said, "but who cares? She's a
good cook. Go on, help yourself."

Clint did so, taking heaping portions of food,
and then a couple of biscuits when Olivia brought
them out. By the time Olivia left the room and he
had enough food in front of him, he decided to
mind his own business where Charles and Anne
Goodnight were concerned.

Goodnight, however, had other ideas.

"She's never shown any inclination to get
involved in my business before," he said.

Clint didn't reply. He didn't think he had to. It
appeared to him that Goodnight was talking as

much to himself as he was to him.

"Then again," the man said, cocking his head to one side, "I've never asked her to, have I?"

No answer. Clint kept his mouth busy chewing bacon, eggs, and biscuits.

"Well," Goodnight said, "maybe it's something to think about . . . later. Meanwhile, I've got something I want to talk to you about."

"What's that?"

"Work."

"Again?" Clint said. "Charles, I thought we settled that—"

"This is a different kind of work, Clint," Goodnight said.

Clint hesitated, then asked, "What did you have in mind?"

"I need someone to look after Annie."

"Look after her? How?"

"I mean protect her," Goodnight said. "Until I find out who wants to kill me, I think she needs a bodyguard."

"Are you offering me the job?" Clint asked.

"Yes," Goodnight said, "and I'll pay you well. She's very important to me. Money is no object."

Clint remained silent and thought about it. First of all, he hadn't intended to stay around for so long, and who knew if and when they'd find out who was behind the attempts to kill Goodnight. Secondly, being around Anne Goodnight all the time—without her husband—didn't seem like that good an idea to him. The attraction between them was too strong, and he didn't think he'd like to test his willpower in that fashion. It would be like taking a man who had stopped drinking and making him work in a saloon.

But then there was Goodnight's last statement, about money being no object. That did have a nice ring to it.

"Well?" Goodnight said. "What do you say?"

Against his better judgment, Clint said, "I can stay a few more days, Charles, but beyond that I'd have to recommend someone else."

"If you did that," Goodnight said, "recommend someone, I mean, would you stay until that person got here?"

Clint frowned.

"Let me think it over, see who I can come up with and when they can get here," he said after a few moments, "and then I can answer that better."

Goodnight nodded and said, "Okay, fair enough. Meanwhile, eat up, then we'll go and introduce you to my neighbor."

# THIRTY-FOUR

By the time they finished breakfast, Anne Goodnight still had not come downstairs. They left the house and Goodnight sought out his foreman, Carl Rivers.

"Carl, Clint and I are going over to talk to Frank Sessions."

"Give me a minute and I'll get some men together," Rivers said immediately.

"No," Goodnight said, "Clint and I will ride over alone."

Rivers frowned and said, "That doesn't sound like a good idea to me, boss."

"Maybe not," Goodnight said, "but Clint's done all right by me so far, hasn't he? I feel safe riding over with him. Meanwhile, there's something else I want you to do for me."

"What's that?"

"Keep an eye on Annie for me, will you?" Goodnight said. "Don't let her stray too far away from the house alone."

"I can do that," Rivers said. "I'll watch over her myself."

"Fine," Goodnight said, touching the man's arm, "I knew I could count on you."

Remembering what Anne had told him about her and the foreman, Clint thought that this might be sort of like sending the fox to guard the chicken coop.

Clint and Goodnight went to the barn, saddled their horses, and then rode out. Goodnight was slightly in the lead as he led the way to the Sessions ranch.


Frank Sessions stepped out onto his front porch and took a deep breath. The plan was for him and his foreman, McCallum, to ride over to the Goodnight ranch this morning to talk to Charles Goodnight. Sessions wanted to find out for himself just what the Gunsmith's role—if he had any— was going to be in the ongoing situation that existed between him and Goodnight.

It was odd how you could be friends with someone for so long, and then that person could quickly become an adversary. Initially, of course, their falling-out was over Anne Perry, who eventually became Anne Goodnight. That soon faded, though, at least for Sessions. He realized that Anne had to choose one or the other, and she made the choice that she thought was the best for her. How could he possibly fault her for doing that— or fault Goodnight for taking her?

Now, however, there was the wire. Sessions *hated* barbed wire, and Charles Goodnight was

trying to ring his land with it. Sessions just didn't
think he could take that lying down. He had to
try to take some action to keep Goodnight from
putting up the wire. He knew that some of their
neighbors felt the same way, but he also knew
that even if he combined his land with that of his
neighbors, Goodnight still had the bigger spread.
Goodnight had the biggest spread in the state,
and while Sessions may have run second to him,
it was by a large margin.

Sessions became aware that McCallum was
walking toward the house from the barn.

"The horses are saddled, boss."

"Good," Sessions said. "Let's get started then. I
want to catch Charles before he starts stringing
wire for the day."

Together they started walking toward the barn,
but they were intercepted by another man.

"What is it, Styles?" McCallum asked.

"Riders comin', boss."

"How many?" McCallum asked.

"Two."

"Do you know who they are?"

"One," the man said, "but not the other."

"Well," Sessions said impatiently, "who is the
one you recognize?"

Styles looked at Sessions and said, "Charles
Goodnight, sir."

Sessions was surprised, but then he looked at
McCallum and said, "Well, it looks like Charles
has gone and saved us a ride."

Both men moved to a point from where they
could see both riders.

"Recognize the other man?" Sessions asked McCallum.

"Yes, sir," McCallum said, "that's Clint Adams."

"The Gunsmith," Sessions said, and McCallum thought he heard something odd in his boss's voice.

Was it awe?

"Should I get some of the other men?" McCallum asked Sessions.

"No," the rancher said, "I don't think they're riding in here to try anything. They're probably just coming to talk."

Both Sessions and McCallum were wearing guns, but Sessions knew that individually or together they would be no match for the Gunsmith.

"Take off your gun," he told McCallum.

"What?"

"I said, take off your gun belt," Sessions said, unbuckling his own.

"What are you doing?" McCallum asked.

Holding his gun belt in his hand, Sessions said, "I don't want to give Adams any reason to think he has to use his gun. Now take yours off."

McCallum did as he was told, and Sessions draped both gun belts over a nearby corral fence, in plain sight. He had just stepped away from both guns when Goodnight and Clint Adams reached them.

# THIRTY-FIVE

As they approached the two men, Clint noticed two things. First, they were unarmed, and second, their gun belts were hanging on the corral fence. Neither man was close enough to the guns to get to them in less than five or six steps. Clint was sure that this was by design.

They knew who he was.

Clint recognized one of the two men as Sam McCallum. He assumed that the other man was Frank Sessions. Sessions was both bigger and older than McCallum, but Clint thought that McCallum was the man in better shape.

"Good morning, Charles," Sessions greeted.

"Frank," Goodnight said.

"You saved me a trip," Sessions said. "I was just on my way out to see you."

"Is that a fact?" Goodnight asked. "About what?"

"Why don't you step down from your horses and we'll talk?" Sessions suggested.

Goodnight and Clint exchanged glances, and then Goodnight said, "Why not?"

He and Clint dismounted. Goodnight walked his horse over to the corral and tied the animal off. Clint simply grounded Duke's reins, allowing the animal to stand on his own.

"Got a lot of faith in that horse, don't you?" Sessions asked.

Clint shrugged.

"He'll go or stay, as he chooses."

"Beautiful animal," the man said. He turned to Goodnight and asked, "What did you want to talk to me about, Charles?"

"What about you?" Goodnight asked. "Why were you coming to see me?"

"Well," Sessions said, "since you saved me the trouble, and technically you're my guest, why don't you go first, huh?"

Goodnight considered the suggestion and then nodded.

"All right, then. There were two attempts on my life recently," Goodnight said.

"So I understand," Sessions said. "Do you know who was responsible?"

"There are a lot of possibilities," Goodnight said, "including you."

"Me?" Sessions said. "Is that why you came? To ask me if I tried to have you killed?"

"That's right."

Sessions stared at Goodnight for a moment and then said, "You've got a lot of nerve coming here and asking me that, Charles."

"Why?" Goodnight asked. "Are you going to tell

me that the thought never entered your mind?"

"No, I'm not going to tell you that," Sessions said. "As a matter of fact, the thought has entered my mind many times."

Goodnight waited for the man to go further and when he didn't, he said, "So?"

"So what?"

"Come on, man!" Goodnight snapped. "What are we talking about here?"

"We're talking about two attempts on your life," Sessions said. "Let me ask you something."

"What?"

"Even if I was responsible, do you think I'd tell you?" Sessions asked.

"I don't know, Frank," Goodnight said. "Would you?"

Sessions thought the question over for a few moments and then said, "You know what? I don't know. I truly don't know if I'd tell you or not."

"So then what you're saying is," Clint said, "that you had nothing to do with the attempts on Mr. Goodnight's life?"

Sessions looked at Clint and said, "Yeah, that's what I'm saying."

"Well, all right, then," Goodnight said. "All I wanted was a straight answer."

"You got it," Sessions said. "That's as straight an answer as I can give you."

"It didn't sound so damned straight to me," Goodnight mumbled.

"I've got a question for you now, Charles," Sessions said.

"All right," Goodnight said, "ask it."

"This man," Sessions said, pointing to Clint.

"What about him?"

"Do you know who he is?"

"Of course I know who he is."

"Does he work for you?"

"No, he does not."

"Then what's he doing here?"

"Mr. Adams is a guest in my house," Goodnight said, "and he simply offered to keep me company on the ride over here."

"Then he's not your hired gun?" Sessions asked.

"No," Goodnight said.

"I'm nobody's hired gun," Clint added.

"So then he's just a friend?"

"That's right, Frank," Goodnight said, "he's just a friend. Not an old friend, but a friend, nevertheless."

Sessions stared at Goodnight for a few moments, flicking his eyes at Clint every so often. Clint knew what was going through his mind. It was very likely that Frank Sessions was dwelling on one of Clint Adams's own most disliked words—coincidence.

As if he had been reading Clint's mind, Sessions said, "That's a little bit of a coincidence, Charles, don't you think?"

"Why do you say that, Frank?" Goodnight asked. "Do you think I was *looking* for a hired gun and Mr. Adams just happened into town?"

"No," Sessions said, "but it is quite a coincidence, isn't it, that he just *happened* to come into town in time to save your life?"

Goodnight nodded and said, "It sure was. It was

a *fortunate* coincidence that he got here in time to save it not once, but twice."

"And did you really think I had something to do with those attempts, Charles?" Sessions asked.

"You have to admit, Frank," Goodnight said, "that you would benefit if I were killed."

"Why? Would that keep the wire from going up?" Sessions asked. "Wouldn't Anne just go ahead and continue, in your memory?"

Goodnight smiled.

"I really can't say what Annie would do in my absence, Frank."

Maybe Goodnight couldn't say what Anne would do, but Clint thought he could. He knew how Anne disliked the wire, and he doubted that she would continue with it if her husband were killed. In fact, she might even—at that point—take down the wire that had already been strung.

"Are we clear on all of this, then?" Goodnight asked Sessions.

"On what?"

"I didn't hire Clint Adams as a hired gunman, and you didn't have anything to do with somebody trying to kill me," Goodnight explained.

Sessions paused a moment, then nodded shortly and said, "That sounds clear."

Goodnight looked at Clint and said, "Well then, I guess we'd better be going."

Both Goodnight and Clint walked to their horses and prepared to mount. As Goodnight put his foot in his stirrup, Sessions called his name.

"What?" Goodnight asked. He paused in that position, but did not turn around.

Clint had already mounted and was watching Frank Sessions and his foreman very carefully.

"Can we talk about the wire again while you're here, Charles?" Sessions asked.

"No," Goodnight said and proceeded to mount his horse. He looked down at Sessions and said, "We've talked enough, Frank. Nothing either of us says is going to change the other one's mind. We both know that."

"So where does that leave us?" Sessions asked.

"The same place we've been for the past several years," Charles Goodnight said. "Going our separate ways."

# THIRTY-SIX

During the ride back to the Goodnight spread from the Sessions ranch Clint was wondering if someone was still following them. They had been followed during the ride there. It felt to him like they were being followed, but that could have been due to the fact that he was expecting to be followed.

"Are we still being kept an eye on?" Charles Goodnight asked him.

"I'm not sure."

"I wonder who it is," Goodnight said, "or was."

"If we knew that," Clint said, "maybe we'd know who was trying to have you killed."

"What should we do?"

Clint thought a moment. He could break off from Goodnight and try to ride back, but the route between the two ranches was largely flat. There was not that much opportunity for cover. Whoever was trailing them would see him in time to be warned. He could try to chase the fellow down, but even with Duke the other man might have enough of a head start to elude him.

"There's not much we can do at this point," Clint said. "But next time . . ."

"What about next time?"

"I don't know," Clint said, "I'm still thinking about it."

In point of fact, the man who had followed them before, and who had followed Clint and Anne Goodnight during their ride, was indeed following them now. When he was sure that they were headed back to the Goodnight ranch, however, he veered off and rode the other way. It was time for him to keep a prearranged meeting with the man who had hired him, to make a report on what he had seen so far.

When Goodnight and Clint returned to the ranch, they were met on the front porch by Anne, who had been sitting out.

"What happened?" she asked.

They dismounted and handed their horses off to one of the ranch hands.

"What's that?" Goodnight asked, indicating the pitcher next to his wife's chair. It was filled with an amber liquid and ice cubes.

"Iced tea," Anne said. "Would you like some?"

"I'd like something a little stronger," her husband replied.

"I'll have some," Clint said. Goodnight looked at him. "It's cold, it's wet, and it will cut through the dust as well as anything else."

Goodnight seemed to think it over for a moment and then said, "All right, I'll have some, too."

Anne poured them both a glass and handed one to each of them. She took her seat again, and her husband sat on the bench next to her. Clint leaned against the front wall of the house.

"So, what happened?" she asked.

"Frank denied that he was behind the attempts to kill me," Goodnight said.

"Did you believe him?"

"I think the question is," Goodnight said, "did Clint believe him?"

"No," Clint said, "I think you should answer the question first."

Goodnight frowned, then took a moment to think. He drank half his iced tea while he was doing so.

"All right," he said finally, "yes, I believe him. I think he was telling the truth."

"So do I," Clint said.

"Then if it's not Frank Sessions," Anne said, "who is it?"

"I don't know," Goodnight said, shrugging. "It could be . . . anyone."

Clint drank his tea thoughtfully. He didn't agree that it could be *anyone*. It had to be someone who would definitely benefit in some way from Goodnight's death.

"I think we have to talk," he said to Goodnight.

"About what?"

"I don't know," Clint said. "Just talk, and see what comes out. Whoever is behind this has something to gain. If you talk about everyone you know, or have done business with, maybe it will become obvious."

"About *everyone?*" Goodnight asked.

Clint looked at him and nodded. "Everyone."

"That could take all day," Goodnight said, "and half the night."

"Maybe," Clint said, "but maybe that means that by morning we'll have an idea who the culprit is."

"He's right, Charles," Anne said.

Goodnight looked at her, and then at Clint.

"So what do we do now?" he asked.

"That's easy," Clint said. "You start talking."

# THIRTY-SEVEN

Lanigan waited impatiently at the prearranged place for the man he'd hired, using Fred Canby's money. It seemed to him that he had been waiting a lot lately, and he was not the kind of man who could do that easily. He preferred action.

He preferred killing, because that was what he did best. Also, it was what Fred Canby paid the most for.

Lanigan wanted Canby to send him after Charles Goodnight and Clint Adams, but the old man wouldn't hear of it.

"I might send you against Goodnight alone, Lanigan," Canby had said, "but not against Adams. Just be patient. I'll get you some help, and then when the time comes, you'll kill one or both of them. We'll see."

Lanigan didn't like that phrase. It seemed to him that was all he used to hear when he was a kid. His mother or his father would say that to him all the time. "We'll see . . . we'll see . . ."

Lanigan didn't want to *see*, he wanted to *do*.

The man riding to meet Lanigan was named Harlan Michaels. Michaels had been working for Goodnight for a few months, but a ranch hand didn't make a lot of money. When he was approached by Lanigan to spy on Charles Goodnight, he agreed. Lanigan was paying him more than twice what he was earning working on the ranch. Taking money from both sides meant he was now making three times as much money as he had before.

He saw Lanigan waiting for him as he approached on his horse, and he got that feeling in the pit of his stomach. Lanigan scared him, because Lanigan had a killer's eyes. Michaels had seen eyes like that before on other men who were killers. Cold, emotionless, expressionless eyes. He figured he'd keep taking Lanigan's money for a while, and when he had enough of a poke saved up, he'd just light out. He didn't want to work for Lanigan much longer.

You never knew with a killer when he'd turn on you and kill *you*.

Lanigan watched Harlan Michaels dismount and walk over, leading his horse.

"What have you got for me, Harlan?" Lanigan asked. His voice was expressionless.

"Not much," Michaels said, then went on to explain how he had followed Adams and Mrs. Goodnight. He told about the incident with the calf and Frank Sessions's men, and then about how he had tailed Goodnight and Adams to the Sessions ranch just that morning.

"That's all?"

"That's it," Michaels said. "Do you, uh, have my money?"

"No," Lanigan said.

"What?"

"You haven't given me anything that's worth money, Harlan," Lanigan said. "In fact, I don't think I need you anymore."

"What?" Michaels said. And as Lanigan drew his gun, the man cried, "Wait, wait, I can get more—"

The sound of the shot drowned him out, and the impact of the bullet in his chest cut him off. He wanted to say something else, but suddenly he couldn't breathe, and he couldn't talk, and then he couldn't see or feel anything at all anymore. . . .

Lanigan rode back to Lubbock and reported to Fred Canby in his office. The older man listened with great interest, especially to the part where Goodnight went to see Sessions.

"I guess he thought Sessions was behind the attempts," Canby said.

"I guess."

"Maybe Frank convinced him that he wasn't," Canby went on. "If that's the case, he'll start looking somewhere else."

"I guess so."

"About Michaels . . ."

"Yes?"

"Did you have to kill him?" Canby asked.

"Yes."

Canby decided not to question Lanigan any further on the subject.

"All right, then," Canby said, "someone came to town today that I want you to meet."

"Who?"

"You'll meet him later today," Canby said. "He's over at the hotel now, resting up. He rode long and hard to get here because I offered him a lot of money to back your play."

"And when do I make my play?"

"Soon," Canby said, "very soon."

Especially if Goodnight was going to start looking elsewhere for the culprit, Canby thought. How long would it be before his old friend realized that he, Fred Canby, had a lot to gain by keeping the range open and free of the barbed wire?

Goodnight and Adams were going to have to be taken care of before that could happen.

# THIRTY-EIGHT

At some point during the night, Clint and Goodnight left the porch of the house and moved into Goodnight's office. They also switched from iced tea to something stronger.

Clint did not try to match Goodnight drink for drink. It occurred to him that the drunker Goodnight got, the looser his talk got. Clint decided that one of them had better be sober enough to remember what Goodnight was saying.

Along around three A.M., Goodnight suddenly stopped talking. Clint had been staring at the floor, listening to the man drone on. When the voice stopped, he looked up and saw that Goodnight's chin had fallen down to his chest. The man had either nodded off or passed out. Either way, Clint decided to carry him up to his bedroom.

He was standing over Goodnight when he realized that carrying him upstairs would mean waking Anne Goodnight, who had turned in some time ago. He decided instead to put Goodnight on one of the sofas in the parlor.

He hoisted the man up onto his shoulder, carried him from the office to the parlor, and set him down gently on a sofa. As soon as he did that, the man began snoring. The sound made Clint realize just how tired he was, as well. He didn't know at that point if Goodnight had said anything of great value, but he decided that morning would be time enough to go through it all again, weeding out what was useless and what was useful. At the moment his brain was just too tired to deal with it.

He left Goodnight where he was and went upstairs to his room.

Clint had just gotten into bed when there was a light knocking at his door. He got out of the bed and, clad only in his underwear, padded barefoot to the door. He opened it a crack and looked out into the hall.

"May I come in?" Anne Goodnight asked.

She was wearing a nightgown—a low-cut nightgown, and he couldn't take his eyes off her breasts.

"I, uh, don't think that's a good idea, Anne," Clint said.

"Why not?" she asked, leaning close. He could smell her now, and his body was reacting of its own accord. "Charles is asleep downstairs, isn't he? Or rather, he's passed out drunk. He's not going to wake up for hours."

"Anne—"

"Please, Clint," she said. "I want to come in and . . . talk."

He hesitated, then said, "All right. Let me get something on."

He left the door ajar and turned to walk to the bed for his pants, but then he heard her enter the room behind him.

"Anne—"

"You don't have to put anything on, Clint," she said, closing the door. "For what I have in mind you don't need to be dressed."

He turned to argue with her and was just in time to see her nightgown fall to the floor in a heap around her lovely ankles.

He opened his mouth to say her name, but no sound came out. She was completely naked, and he couldn't help but drink in the sight of her. Her breasts were full, almost pear-shaped, and the nipples were dark and erect. She had a small waist, which made her hips seem even wider than they were. Her thighs were full, and her calves firm. She was a big woman, all right, as he had suspected each time he saw her dressed. Now, naked, there could be no doubt.

And there was also no doubt about what it was she had in mind. He didn't want to do it, but his body was not listening to his mind—and she knew it.

She walked across the room to him and put her hands on his bare chest.

"You want me, don't you?" she asked.

She slid her hands down his torso, over his belly, and then reached between his legs.

"Yes," she said, "I see you do want me, just as I want you."

"No," he said, but she did not believe him.

"Yes," she said, "oh yes . . ."

She was almost as tall as he was, and she only had to lean up a little to kiss him. As she did so, she slid her hand inside his underwear to take hold of him. He growled into her mouth, deciding that if this was what she wanted, then she might as well get it—and he might as well enjoy it. He'd worry about the consequences afterward.

He put his arms around her and pulled her to him, kissing her deeply. His tongue entered her mouth and she moaned. Using both hands she slid his underwear down until it fell to the floor and there was nothing between them. She moaned again as he slid his hands down her back to cup her buttocks.

Squeezing her marvelously firm and smooth butt in his hands, he turned her and pushed her back toward the bed. When the backs of her thighs struck the mattress she fell onto it, taking him with her.

On the bed he began to explore her body with not only his hands, but his mouth as well. Her moans and cries increased in volume, but neither of them worried about that. Charles Goodnight was well beyond hearing them.

He worked his way down her body until he was nestled between her legs, his mouth and tongue working avidly.

"Oh my God, yes!" she cried. "Oh please, oh yes, Clint . . . yes!"

She began to buck beneath him as waves of pleasure flooded over her, and then he raised himself above her and plunged into her. He groaned as her heat surrounded him. He had his knees outside of her legs, and she seemed incredibly tight as he worked himself in and out of her.

She reached down with one hand to press against his leg, and he thought he knew what she wanted. He lifted one knee, and then the other, until he was now kneeling inside her thighs. He drove into her more deeply that way, and although she wasn't as tight in this position, she was still very hot and wet. She brought her legs up, then, to wrap them around his waist, and also encircled him with her arms. She brought him tightly against her, so that her mouth was right against his ear as she moaned and cried out. They moved together, the tempo increasing until they were both grunting and sweating with the effort.

He felt the rush building up inside of him, as if it was welling up from his ankles, through his legs and thighs into his groin. He knew he was going to explode inside of her, and he didn't want to, not just yet. He controlled it and continued to move with her until her cries became such that he knew she was very near her climax . . . and that was when he released the control he had over himself and allowed his explosion to happen. . . .

# THIRTY-NINE

"Well," Clint said later, "this was a mistake."

Lying next to him, exhausted, Anne Goodnight asked, "Do you really think that?"

"Yes," Clint said. "Oh, I'm not saying it wasn't wonderful, Anne, but it definitely was a mistake. Aside from that it was just plain wrong."

"That's the way you look at it," Anne said. "To my way of thinking, it was just right."

"How do you figure that?"

She stretched, and he was glad that the sheet was covering her. He knew he wouldn't be able to resist her now any more than he had the first time. Actually, he was wishing she'd get dressed and go back to her own room.

"I needed this, Clint," she said. "I needed you, here, tonight. It doesn't mean I don't love my husband, and it doesn't mean that it will ever happen again."

"Oh, it won't," he said. "I can promise you that."

"Really?" she said. Suddenly her hand was on

him, and he was swelling again. "Never again?" she asked as she stroked him gently.

"No," he said, turning and reaching out for her, "never . . . not after tonight."

In the middle of the night Fred Canby suddenly sat up in his bed. The move was so abrupt that it woke the young woman who was sleeping next to him. She was still there, despite the fact that he had been unable to perform with her. He had told her that he still wanted her to sleep with him, and she didn't mind. She was still getting paid, and she didn't even have to service him.

"What is it?" she asked.

"Nothing," he said. "Go back to sleep."

He swung his feet to the floor, reached for his robe, put it on, and left the bedroom. He went to his office and poured himself a drink.

He wasn't sure what had awakened him. He didn't think it had been a dream. At least, he didn't remember any dream. All he knew was that he had awakened with the sudden knowledge that today was the day that Charles Goodnight and Clint Adams had to be taken care of. In the morning he would call for Lanigan and give him his instructions. He and the new man would go out and kill both Goodnight and Adams today. By nightfall, both men had to be dead, and business as usual could go on for Fred Canby. He had open range to claim and then sell, which he could not do if Goodnight's wire was in the way.

First he'd get rid of Goodnight, and after that the damned wire would come down.

• • •

Anne Goodnight left Clint's bed at about four A.M. and went back to her own room. She seemed very content, and not regretful in the least. He, too, was physically content, but mentally he was somewhat less than that.

He had slept with his host's wife. He wasn't sure yet that he and Goodnight were friends, but that still did not excuse his behavior.

He stood up, walked to the window, and looked out at the grounds in front of the house. He truly wished that he had never stopped in Lubbock, but now the damage was done. Besides, if he hadn't stopped in Lubbock, there was a good chance that Charles Goodnight would now be dead. He shook his head. There was no way to change this. He certainly would not trade Goodnight's death for this not to have happened. He was just going to have to deal with it.

He went back to bed, wondering how Anne would feel in the morning. Would she regret what had happened? Would she be unable to meet his eyes with hers? Would Goodnight notice that something was amiss?

Clint decided that maybe tomorrow was the day he should leave—and when he did, he would ride *around* Lubbock as he headed south, not through it.

# FORTY

Fred Canby watched Lanigan and the new man, whose name was Myles, Douglas Myles. He preferred to be called Myles, though. Canby marveled at how alike the two men were. Both preferred to be called by their last names. Both were quiet, seemingly emotionless men— and both were killers.

Myles had a reputation for getting the job done, which was why Canby had sent for him.

The main difference between the two men was physical. Lanigan was very tall and thin,— bony. Myles was under six feet, stocky, easily outweighing Lanigan by fifty pounds.

When the two men had met in the saloon the day before, they had studied each other warily. Canby knew that Lanigan and Myles would never be friends, probably never even like each other. That didn't matter to him. All they had to do was work together for a day or two, and then they could go their separate ways once more.

Canby was of the opinion that, left in the same place too long, one would most certainly kill the other. It was simply their nature.

"All right," Canby said, "today is the day."

"Today?" Lanigan said.

"That's right."

Lanigan frowned. If it was to be today, they would have to ride hard to get there. A man on a horse, riding nonstop, could make it by late afternoon. It was only when you were burdened—the way Goodnight had been with the wagonload of wire—that it was an overnight trip.

"All right, then," Lanigan said. "Today it is."

"Well, good," Myles said around a wooden match. "I was afraid I was gonna have to stay here longer."

"You don't like it here?" Lanigan asked.

Myles gave Lanigan a heavy lidded look and removed the match from his mouth.

"No, I don't."

"What's wrong with it?"

Myles smiled humorlessly and said, "I don't much like the people."

"Anybody in particular?" Lanigan asked, bristling.

"That's enough . . . gentlemen," Canby said. "As long as I'm paying you, I'd prefer that you do your bickering on your own time."

Myles still smiled, but he placed the matchstick back into his mouth and looked at Canby.

"You're the boss," he said. Then he added, "For now."

"That is correct," Canby said. Neither man

frightened him exactly, but he felt uncomfortable in their presence.

"Where do you want it done?" Lanigan asked.

"I don't care where or how," Canby said, "I only care that it be today."

"You want both of them?" Myles asked.

"I want Goodnight," Canby said. "I don't much care what happens to Adams. He's yours if you want him."

"That'd be a feather in my cap," Myles said, "killing the Gunsmith."

"Who says *you're* gonna kill him?" Lanigan asked.

Myles looked at him and said, "You sayin' you can take him?"

"You think I can't?"

"Gentlemen," Canby said, "if you please. I'd prefer that you don't kill each other until after you have taken care of my business?"

Lanigan and Myles both looked at him, and Canby squirmed in his seat, wondering if he had gone too far.

"He's got a good point," Lanigan finally said.

"Yes, he does," Myles said.

"Let's get to it, then," Lanigan said.

They both stood up and headed for the door. Canby held his breath as they reached the door together, wondering if they were going to argue over who would go through it first. They did not. Lanigan opened the door and allowed Myles to precede him. As the door closed behind them, Canby expelled a sigh of relief.

# FORTY-ONE

That morning at breakfast Clint was very surprised at Anne Goodnight's behavior. She chattered away with her husband and with him, and not once did Clint see any hint of discomfort on her part. As for him, he had come downstairs with feelings of dread, but it soon became clear to him that they were unwarranted.

Goodnight himself was another surprise. For a man who had drunk as much as he had the night before and passed out, he was surprisingly chipper.

"All right," he finally said at one point, "enough idle chatter. Tell me, Clint, did my drunken ramblings last night reveal anything?"

It was odd, but that morning when he had awakened, Clint realized almost immediately that Goodnight had indeed said something that was of value.

"Who is Fred Canby again?"

"Fred?" Goodnight said. "He's a local businessman. Owns a small ranch, mostly for show."

"Is that all?"

"Well, no . . . he has some political ambitions, Fred does. Why?"

"Is he a friend of yours?"

"I consider him, a friend, yes," Goodnight said. "I've known him a long time."

"How does he feel about the wire?"

"He's against it," Goodnight said.

"How strong is his opposition?"

"Fairly strong, I guess, but see, he's not a rancher, so his opposition is moral."

"Is it?" Clint asked.

"What do you mean?"

"What if his opposition was political?"

"I don't understand."

"What if 'Open Range' was his platform for running for office?" Clint asked.

"Clint, do you know much about politics?"

"Very little."

"Then you don't understand that the people who would support Fred are the big ranchers, the cattlemen. Like me," Goodnight explained.

Clint frowned.

"Then I *really* don't understand politics," Clint said. "If he needs your support, why would he oppose you on the wire issue?"

Now it was Goodnight's turn to stop short.

"I don't know," Goodnight said.

"In your opinion," Clint asked, "are the big ranchers going to be largely in favor of the wire, or will they be against it?"

"I think Frank Sessions will be in the minority,"

Goodnight said. "The big ranchers are going to want to fence off their land, and the barbed wire is the perfect way to do that and be sure that no one is going to trespass."

"Then I'll ask you again. Why is Fred Canby opposed to it?"

Goodnight frowned and said, "I don't know."

"This is just a theory," Clint said, "but what if Canby is buying up land around here?"

"I'd know about it."

"Not if he had someone doing it for him," Clint said.

"Are you leading up to accusing Fred of trying to have me killed?"

"I don't know what I'm leading up to, Charles," Clint said. "It just struck me as odd that someone who would be after your support would be opposing you on an issue as important as this."

"Now that you mention it," Goodnight said, "it does seem odd. Maybe we should ride into Lubbock and ask him, huh?"

"Maybe we should," Clint said.

"Then we'll do that right after breakfast."

"There's something else," Clint said.

"What?"

"From Lubbock I'll be continuing on," Clint said. "It's time for me to leave."

That drew him a look from Anne, one which Goodnight did not see.

"Well," Goodnight said, "I think I've done everything I can to get you to stay. I've offered you every job I have to offer."

"I appreciate the offers, Charles," Clint said,

"but it's time . . . that's all."

"I understand," Goodnight said. "When I was younger, I was that way. You just stay in one place too long and you get the urge to move on. I appreciate everything *you've* done for *me*, Clint."

"I was glad to help, Charles," Clint said, feeling a great surge of guilt over what he had done last night.

"We'll be sorry to see you go, Clint," Anne said, looking right at him. "Now who will ride with me in the mornings?"

"I think Charles should," Clint said.

"If I only had time—" Goodnight started, but Clint cut him off.

"Make time, Charles," he said. Goodnight looked at him sharply and Clint added, "You've got a lovely wife. Make time for her. She's the one who's going to support you no matter what."

Goodnight stared at Clint, then turned his head and looked at Anne, who smiled at him. Suddenly, Goodnight covered his wife's hand with his.

"You might have something there, Clint," the man said. "You just might have something there."

# FORTY-TWO

Clint Adams and Charles Goodnight left the Goodnight ranch on horseback at the same time Lanigan and Myles left Lubbock. It was destined, then, that they would meet halfway.

"I was just thinking about what you said this morning," Goodnight said.

They had been riding at a good clip for a few hours and were almost at the halfway point between the ranch and Lubbock.

"About Canby?"

"Well, that too," Goodnight said, "but I was thinking more about what you said about Annie."

"Oh."

"I think you're right," Goodnight said. "I haven't given her enough attention. In fact, at times I've just downright neglected her."

"Well," Clint said, "she's still there for you, isn't she?"

"Yep, she sure is," Goodnight said, "but it's taken you to make me realize it. Tell me, what makes you so smart all the time?"

"I'm not smart *all* the time," Clint said. "In fact, I don't think I'm too smart *most* of the time."

If he was, Clint thought, he wouldn't keep getting himself in these kinds of messes.

"I say we take Adams out first," Myles said.

"He's not the target," Lanigan argued.

They had been riding along, pushing their horses for quite a while, and were now approaching the halfway point between Lubbock and the Goodnight ranch.

"Maybe not," Myles said, "but he's the one who's gonna be the hardest to handle."

"Still," Lanigan said, "he ain't the one we're bein' *paid* for."

"Maybe not," Myles said, "but he's the one who can *keep* us from gettin' paid."

"Okay," Lanigan said, after a moment. "Okay, so if they're together, we'll have to take him first. That makes sense."

"I know it does."

"But if they're *not* together, then we'll take care of Goodnight first," Lanigan said. "I want to make damned sure I do what I'm gettin' paid to do."

Now Myles took a moment to think, and then said, "Sounds fair."

Lanigan looked over at Myles, who was looking straight ahead. Lanigan didn't trust the other man. He thought that Myles was in this for more than just the money. He was in this for the glory that killing the Gunsmith would bring him.

Lanigan's first and only allegiance in this life was to money. If killing Clint Adams brought him more recognition, he'd simply be able to command more money for his services. He did nothing just for the glory of it, and he felt that men who did were dangerous.

Myles was dangerous. Lanigan wouldn't put it past Myles to try to kill him after they finished with Goodnight and Adams.

That meant that Lanigan was going to have to kill Myles before Myles could kill him.

That was something that was going to have to be timed just right.

# FORTY-THREE

"What's that?" Goodnight asked.

Clint peered into the distance and said, "If I'm not mistaken, it's a body. Let's take a look."

They rode up to it, and as they approached, they could clearly see that it was indeed a body.

They dismounted, walked over to it, and turned the corpse over.

"Know him?" Clint asked.

"I sure do," Goodnight said. "He works for me. His name is—or was—Harlan Michaels. Carl told me he sent this fella into Lubbock to see if Terry Lester was well enough to ride back."

Clint studied the body.

"He must have been bushwhacked," Goodnight said.

"He was shot at close range from the front, not the back," Clint said. He checked the ground and said, "There was someone here with him. Look here."

Goodnight took a look and saw a horse's hoofprint with a half-moon cutout in it.

"What are you thinking?" Goodnight asked.

"Just that maybe he was meeting somebody here to talk to them, give them some information."

"About us?"

Clint nodded.

"You're thinking that this is the man who was tailing us, keeping tabs on us for . . . for who?"

"For whoever," Clint said. "Besides, he wasn't the first of your men to be bought, was he?"

"Jesus," Goodnight said, passing his hand over his forehead, pushing his hat back on his head, "maybe I ought to start paying my men more."

"Maybe," Clint said, "or maybe you should be more careful about who you hire."

"You want to bury him?" Goodnight asked.

Clint wasn't listening, though—not to Goodnight, anyway.

"What is it?" Goodnight asked.

"Riders coming."

"I don't hear—"

"Listen!"

Goodnight listened, and then suddenly he heard them. Horses were approaching at a gallop.

"How many?" he asked.

"Two, I think," Clint said.

"What should we do?" Goodnight asked. "Take cover?"

"No," Clint said. "Let's just stand our ground and see who it is. It may be nothing, but spread out a little, anyway." He pointed and said, "They'll probably come over that rise. Let's be ready for anything."

As they approached the rise, Lanigan suddenly realized that they were near the place where he had met and killed Harlan Michaels.

He and Myles topped the rise, and where Lanigan expected to see Harlan Michaels's body instead he saw the body—and two men.

"Hold it!" he shouted to Myles, who reined his horse in hard.

"What is it?" Myles asked.

"Those two men."

"I see 'em," Myles said. "Who are they?"

"That's Charles Goodnight and Clint Adams. Adams is on your left."

Myles looked surprised, then pleased. He licked his lips, the way a man facing a big dinner might.

"Well," he said, "it looks like they're gonna make this easy for us. Have they ever seen you?"

"Goodnight has, around town."

"Does he know you work for Canby?"

"I don't know," Lanigan said. "I can't be sure."

"Well, they're starin' up at us and we're starin' down at them. Nothin's gonna get done this way."

"What do you suggest?" Lanigan asked.

"I say we ride down there nice and easy like, and then throw down on them."

"That's the Gunsmith down there, Myles," Lanigan reminded him.

"So?" Myles said. "We both take him first, that's all."

"He might get one of us," Lanigan said.

Myles smiled and said, "That'll mean that one of us will get paid and one of us won't. You worried it might be me and not you?"

"The hell with it," Lanigan said tightly. "Let's go do it."

"They're coming down," Clint said. "Do you know either one of them?"

"I can't be sure from this distance," Goodnight said, "but the one on the left looks like a man I've seen in town."

"Who?"

"His name's Lanigan."

"What's he do?"

"Not much," Goodnight said. "He's just always around. Works for people here and there."

"Has he ever worked for Canby?"

Goodnight hesitated, then said, "You know, I think he has . . . as a matter of fact, I'm sure of it. Lanigan came into the Americana Saloon once, and Fred commented that the man had his uses."

"Well," Clint said, "remembering that might have just given us the edge we need, Charles."

"I'm not a gunman, Clint," Goodnight said. "I mean, I'll back you, but I just want you to know that."

"When the shooting starts, hit the ground and

roll," Clint said. "If you're moving, it'll be harder for them to hit you."

"And just about impossible for me to hit them."

Clint looked at him and said, "Just do it, leave the rest to me."

# FORTY-FOUR

The two riders approached, and Clint kept his eyes on both of them. Luckily, they were riding close together. When they started to move apart, it would signal that they were ready to make their move. He only hoped that Goodnight wouldn't give in to nervousness and do something stupid.

"Looks like you fellas have had some trouble," Lanigan said.

"Not us," Clint said, "this fella. We just found him that way."

"Gonna bury him?" Lanigan asked.

"No," Clint said. "Maybe you want to."

"Why would I?"

Clint decided to take a wild shot and said, "Maybe because you killed him."

The other man moved his horse away from Lanigan's as Lanigan said, "Shit," and went for his gun.

"Now!" Clint shouted at Goodnight.

Goodnight hit the ground and rolled to his left, clawing for his gun.

Clint drew swiftly and fired at Lanigan. The bullet shattered Lanigan's right collarbone, numbing his arm so that the gun dropped from it.

Myles had his gun out, but Goodnight was firing, and although his shots were going wild, they were enough to attract Myles's attention. Clint took advantage of the situation and fired at the man. His bullet struck Myles square in the chest, punching right through his breastbone and driving all of his breath out of him.

Lanigan, his right arm useless, was having trouble with his horse, which had been spooked by the shots. Suddenly the horse reared and Lanigan fell off, dropping backward and hitting the ground with his back. He lay there motionless, unable to move because of the pain in his arm and the fact that all of the breath had been knocked out of him.

"Easy!" Clint shouted to Goodnight, who was staggering to his feet. "It's all over."

Clint walked over to Myles and checked him to make sure he was dead. After making certain of that, he walked over to Lanigan, who was still breathing. The man was lying on his back, and his eyes were open, but he didn't seem able to move.

"Keep an eye on him," Clint said to Goodnight.

"Right."

Clint rounded up the two men's horses and checked their hooves. Sure enough, the horse that Lanigan had been riding had a half-moon shape cutout in the hoof of his left foreleg.

"Well," Clint said, "we can be pretty sure he killed Michaels. Now let's find out for sure who he works for."

Clint hunkered down next to the injured man, who was just beginning to breathe normally.

"Hurts," the man gasped at the pain in his shoulder from the shattered collarbone.

Clint inspected the wound and saw shards of white bone showing through the skin.

"Looks bad, all right," he said. "You need a doctor."

"Doctor—"

"Nearest one's in Lubbock, I guess."

The man closed his eyes, and for a moment Clint thought he had passed out, but then he opened them again.

"We can get you to the doctor, Lanigan," Clint said, "but there's a price."

"W-what . . . price?"

"The name of the man you work for," Clint said. "The name of the man who sent you to kill Charles Goodnight."

There was a pause, and then the man said, "Can't. . . ."

Clint reached down with his hand and touched the tip of a bone that was protruding. He hardly touched it really, but the pain that it caused must have been considerable. The man gasped, arched his back, and almost passed out.

"The name, Lanigan, and we'll get you to a doctor," Clint said.

Lanigan closed his eyes, and Clint waited. He had either passed out or was trying to decide what to do. Finally, he opened his eyes.

"C-Canby," he said weakly, "F-Fred Canby. N-now . . . doctor. . . ."

"Sure, Lanigan," Clint said, "we'll get you to a doctor."

He stood up and looked at Goodnight.

"Goddamn!" Goodnight said. "Fred Canby?"

"I guess we better get Lanigan into Lubbock, and then we can get the sheriff and have Canby arrested. Then you can ask Canby why."

Goodnight was shaking his head.

"It doesn't much matter why, Clint," he said. "It's enough that he tried to kill me. The why of it really isn't that important."

"Well," Clint said, "with Lanigan still alive, we can prove that it was Canby, so I guess you can stop looking over your shoulder."

"No," Goodnight said sadly. "After this I'll be looking over my shoulder even more, at my men, my neighbors, my friends. . . ."

"Well," Clint said, realizing that he had lived most of his life that way, "it never hurts to be too careful, does it?"

Watch for

**GILLETT'S RANGERS**

145th novel in the exciting GUNSMITH series
from Jove

*Coming in January!*

# J. R. ROBERTS

# THE

# GUNSMITH